The Death of Sheherzad

THE INDIA LIST

The Death of Sheherzad

INTIZAR HUSAIN

Translated by
Rakshanda Jalil

LONDON NEW YORK CALCUTTA

SERIES EDITOR

Arunava Sinha

Seagull Books, 2016

First published in India in 2014 by Harper Perennial
An imprint of HarperCollins *Publishers*

Printed in arrangement with HarperCollins *Publishers*.
This edition is not for sale in the Indian subcontinent (India, Pakistan,
Sri Lanka, Bangladesh, Nepal, Bhutan, Myanmar and the Maldives),
Singapore, Malaysia and the UAE.

ISBN 978 0 8574 2 393 1

British Library Cataloguing-in-Publication Data
A catalogue record for this book is available from the British Library.

Typeset in 15/15.3 Adobe Arabic by Jojy Philip, New Delhi, India
Printed and bound by Hyam Enterprises, Calcutta, India

To Najmi

Contents

Circle[1]

It is as though someone is urging me to rake the ashes. Compelled, I sit down to sift the fifty-year-old ashes. What is left to explore? But I have the bad habit of scouring the past. Some dusty alleys, some half-grimy faces, some voices, a mildewed parapet, a tumbled-down turret, a few trees, birds – that's all that appears in my mind's eye. Gradually, a tableau unfolds: a shop front, some people sitting and chatting on the shop's stoop, the shopowner standing behind a huge cauldron of milk, stirring its boiling contents with a ladle. The scene is straight out of my very first story. It comes back to me now with the realization that something is lacking here. In fact, this isn't the story I had wanted to write. Most important of all, the main character is missing from this story. Qayyuma was not the central figure of this story.

It was someone else. I don't know how I could have forgotten that while writing my story. I remember it now, fifty years later. I can clearly remember that whole set of characters

---

[1] Published as 'Daira' in the short story collection titled *Sheherzad ke Naam*, Sang-e-Meel Publications, Lahore, 2002.

and that group of people sitting and chatting at the shop front. Those days my mind had become so hazy. It is only now, after so many years, that my memory has become nimble again. Now, those pictures are emerging clearly before my eyes.

Should I rewrite the story I had written fifty years ago? I remember something that Karn had said. In the forests of Khando, Arjun had slain the serpent that was Ashwasen's mother. When Karn aimed his arrow at Arjun, Ashwasen thought it was a good opportunity to avenge his mother's death. He slithered up from the bowels of the earth and wrapped himself around Karn's arrow. But by a single stroke, Lord Krishan caused Karn's chariot to get stuck in the mud at that very moment, and Karn's arrow went to naught. The serpent, Ashwasen, beseeched Karn to let him entwine himself once again around his arrow and shoot Arjun once more. But Karn said he did not believe in re-using an arrow that had once left his bow. If the arrow was wasted, so be it; that was its destiny. I am lost in thought ... should I attempt to rewrite the story that has been squandered already? After much dilly-dallying, I make up my mind. Karn's words went away with him. I must attempt to write that story once again.

No, now this story has gotten away from you. Now someone else will write it.

I hear these words and am confounded. Where did these words come from? Who said them? Did they come from within the story or from one of its dramatis personae? Well, never mind. Someone else can also write this story. But it must be written once again. Who will write it? Anybody else can do the job. I wasn't the only one who was present at the time. There were scores of others. Though everyone else had left at some point or the other, save for that one person. So, who will be the 'other'? I am the only 'other'. Now, I shall write this story. Yes, I. Even though I am one of those who left; all the others have made new homes in new lands. I was the only one who never found peace and tranquility. Sometimes I am seized by doubt. Have I left that place or not? It seems as though that other person has got left behind, and the rest have all come here. And I, I am neither here nor there. Like a restless spirit. Anyhow, I am not about to tell my story here. I have to tell the story of the person who is the central character of that story.

Before I begin my story, I must first outline the map of that town for you. But before I explain that to you, you too must understand that towns are not just about geography; neither are they just a cluster of dwellings rooted in solid earth. A part of them is on the ground, the rest inside one's mind and soul. And that is why there is no point in giving the geographical name of that town. Of course, you can see the town as it stands with your eyes, but there is far more to it than that which meets the eye. I have seen the town in so many guises that I have started calling it Guisetown.[2] And

---

[2] In the original story, Intizar Husain has called it Roopnagar. Roopnagar, from the description in the story, can be any small town anywhere in Uttar Pradesh, though there is a Roopnagar in Delhi and another in Punjab. Roopnagar is also a metaphor in popular culture for any generic town, especially a pretty town. I have chosen to translate it as Guisetown because the word 'roop' also has an element of form, forms that can change, hence a town of guises.

what a town it was! I mean, on the surface it was like any
other town, colourless and drab, as is the destiny of all small
towns. There used to be such a crowd in the grocer's market.
The air would be heavy with the pungent smell of asafoetida.
Sacks of asafoetida, turmeric, chilly and salt would be piled
inside the shops. You could find everything there. When
pulao or qorma had to be cooked at home for special guests,
I would buy cardamom, mace, nutmeg and saffron wrapped
in scraps of paper from this very market. But the big market
would be even more crowded, what with bales of cotton
stacked in piles and carts laden with grain and slabs of raw
jaggery jostling for space. And such a crowd of buyers that
God save you from that crush of people! It wasn't so much
the buyers as the slabs of jaggery that took up all the space.
And among them were sparrows and pigeons, also a few
partridges. If you wanted to see a bigger crowd, you could
go to the open-air market beside the pond. The place was so
full of dirt that by evening a film of dust coated the radishes,
turnips, cauliflowers, cabbages, pumpkins, spinach, potatoes
and an assortment of greens and vegetables.

The pond would be full of water only during the
monsoon. What a large and deep pond that was, with steps
on all sides. It looked like a large overflowing sea. In the
monsoons, its water became green. In the summer, its water
sank to the lowest step, and clouds of dust billowed all
around it as the water completely disappeared. In its dry
days, the pond was distinguished by the two bulls that were
usually found standing inside it. One was a dirty white,
the other black. They stood in splendid silence: one on the

right edge of the pond, the other on the far left. The dirty white bull was more fretful; he would begin to snort and paw for no reason. Sometimes he would rush towards the big market, snorting and hissing. He had such an awesome presence, the crowd would part, like a layer of algae on the surface of a pond, and he would rush through with complete disregard. Sometimes the black bull too would get restless. He would get out of the pond with measured, imperious steps and walk, snorting and bellowing all the way, towards the grocer's market, and then towards the open market and the gaggle of small shops.

Talking about the cluster of shops reminds me that once the two bulls had come face to face with each other here. It had seemed like the end of the world. There they stood, with their horns locked in mortal combat. How far the white bull had pushed the black one! But when the black bull pushed back, all the sweet-laden trays at Mitthan Lal's halwai shop were overturned. So you can imagine.

Mitthan Lal was one of a kind. His gujiya was so fantastic that peda-makers from Mathura and Badayun would come to kiss his hands. How grand his shop looked on the eve of Diwali. Trays laden with sweets rose in tiers from the floor to the ceiling. You could find just about every type of sweet here – from gujiya to tangani.

And what could you find at Qayyuma's shop? Only pedas. And those too were no match for Mitthan Lal's pede and gujiya. Anyway, this was not a marketplace. This was the only shop in front of Hafiz-ji's chaupal. So there was never any hustle-bustle here. Though, every six months or so, or on special occasions, you could hear the cry 'Ram naam satya hai, Ram naam satya hai'. And a dead body would be rushed by on its funeral pyre. Following close behind would be a group of Hindu mourners, clutching the firewood for the pyre and chanting their prayers for the dead. This was a Muslim neighbourhood, but still nothing much could be done since the way to the cremation ground went through this mohalla. No other Hindu procession or party ever came this way. Hindu marriage parties, which were led by horses festooned with kite-paper and tinsel streamers, would come right up till the edge of the lane, then turn left towards the Red Temple Lane. The wedding procession of Ramchandar-ji would also duck into this lane. All those who sat on Qayyuma's shop front had to get up and come to the edge of the lane to watch the elephant with the red and yellow checks painted on its forehead carrying the howdah in which Raja Ramchandar-ji, the groom, and Sita-ji, his bride, sat dressed in their wedding finery. All those who wanted to play Holi also took the same route.

The largest of all Hindu parades and pageants was Ramchandar-ji's wedding procession. Only one other procession had been bigger than that. That had been when Master Piyare Lal had courted arrest. There had been such a crowd here, and such an angry one at that, that had they stormed the police station they would have torn the policemen from limb to limb. The police, too, had their guns trained. Master Piyare Lal had paused before entering the police station and addressed the crowd. 'Friends, don't forget the words of Mahatma Gandhi. We don't talk about an armed revolution; we only advocate non-violence. This is what Gandhi-ji has taught us. This is our belief and therein lies the key to the success and happiness of our people. Mahatma Gandhi ki ...' And the crowd roared 'Jai!' The air was rent with jubilant cries of 'Inquilab Zindabad!' and 'Mahatma Gandhi ki Jai!' Master Piyare Lal folded his hands and said 'Namaste' to the crowd and entered the police station. The massive iron-barred gate clanged shut behind him. After the historic battle of the bulls, this was the second major event in the lives of those who lived here.

Only one procession went past Qayyuma's shop. And it wasn't a particularly large one either. It was the procession of the saint Shah Madaar's rods. They weren't exactly rods. There would be just one long staff-like thing, as long as the tallest alam. It would be carried to the accompaniment of drums and cymbals. A dervish-looking person would walk alongside, wearing green robes. He had long, unkempt hair and wore a yellow and red string around his neck. He was the keeper of Shah Madaar's shrine. He would plant the staff in front of Uncle Farooq's gate. The drums and cymbals would begin to beat furiously. And some kind soul would come and start distributing malida.

There, I nearly forgot to tell you about the big procession. The zuljinah procession took the same route too. After all, the way to the Karbala also went through here. If you went straight ahead, you reached the ruined Chamunda. If you turned left and walked up a little, you could see the moss-covered spires of Karbala. But let me not talk about Karbala now. If I go that way again, I will never return. But

there is no harm in going towards the Chamunda. I used to
roam around a lot near its ruined ramparts. I have kicked
dust from here till the little bridge on many a scorching
afternoon. Drained by the heat and unable to take another
step, I would often go and sit on the roof of the Chamunda
temple where an ancient peepal tree gave respite from the
relentless sun. This was the only sheltering tree for miles
around. Not a single banyan, mango or tamarind tree grew in
this wilderness. The ruins of Chamunda further added to its
desolation. It must have been a large temple a long time ago,
but time had not been kind to it. A few broken-down, moss-
encrusted walls and a roof were all that remained. Under
the roof was an idol that, as far as I could remember, had
not seen any fresh offerings of flowers. Behind it stretched
the eerie stillness of the cremation ground. One never knew
when a corpse was brought here or when it was burnt. At
least on those blistering afternoons, one never saw another
human being around. Though, if you sat under the shade
of the peepal tree on the roof of the Chamunda, you could
see a few ploughmen in the distance, digging at the base of
the yellow dunes and loading the dun-coloured earth onto
donkeys. From this vantage point, that scene looked like it
belonged to some other world. You never ever saw another
human face near the ruined temple. There would be just us
and a few monkeys dangling from the branches of the peepal
tree. But we were never scared. It was only at night, when
we heard the call of the jackals coming from the direction of
the Chamunda, that we were frightened. In the silence of the
night, their howling could make my heart thud with terror

as I lay in bed. Listening to those calls, I used to imagine that all the jackals from the neighbouring jungles had gathered atop the Chamunda and were baying with their snouts turned towards our homes.

It was only once that I had felt scared during the day. But I wasn't the only one. There were a whole lot of us. On a blistering hot afternoon, we had come out of the Chamunda and were shuffling along the dirt track when Shaddu suddenly spoke up in a wonderstruck voice: 'A woman!'

'A woman,' we stopped in our tracks and chorused, 'where?'

'There she goes.'

A little further ahead, a woman was walking beside the dirt track. She was wearing a pale red ghagra, a matching blouse, and had a ring in her nose and large hoops in her ears.

'You twits, that isn't a woman.'

'Then who is she?'

'Look at her feet; you will know for yourself.'

And when we turned to look, she was gone.

'But where did she go?'

At that very moment, a kite soaring in the sky let out a raucous caw. It was a strange keening sound; it seemed to scratch the air around us.

'Run.'

And we ran from there. The kite's screech followed us for a long while. Why am I narrating this in the past tense? That scene is frozen in time. I had gone down that track just a few days go. After all, how long has it been since I saw my last dream? In my dream, I had seen everything just as it used to be. If anything, it looked brighter. Or at least, so it seemed to me. It is only now, much later, that I am able to look at that scene in minute detail. I do believe that things reveal their true self only in dreams. Walls and niches, streets and alleys, plants and trees, the earth and the sky – it is only after we stop seeing them with our eyes that we truly begin to see them, when they start coming in our dreams and calling out to us. First in the first dream, then in the second, then the third and so on. It is after so many dreams that my town has come completely alive before my eyes, and I am now able to see it fully.

See it fully … I said that wrong. I have still not seen it fully. For, you see, I have still not been to Karbala. How I love going in that direction! Just as I approach it, God knows what happens, I wake up. The map of my town is incomplete if it does not include Karbala. That used to be the high point of our town. You could say you have mapped the town fully only after you have been to Karbala. It is always the last stop on my journey of enchantment. On those long, silent afternoons which never seemed to end, we would trudge through the dusty alleys of our neighbourhood, walk from the Chamunda right up till the little bridge, and then as we turned to trace our steps back, one or the other of us would pipe up, 'Yaar, shall we go to Karbala?' And it was as though we had spoken up in unison, from deep within our hearts. And our feet would immediately turn in that direction. From the Chamunda, we would go past the old fort. And as we rounded the mound near the old fort, we would come upon the fields belonging to Sheikh Maddu where a Persian wheel would be slowly spinning. Just a little further grows a red tamarind tree and beyond that lies Babwa the wrestler's wrestling pit. After Babwa's wrestling pit, there is a tangle of berry bushes, then the white man's grave, and then the orchard belonging to the Sambhali family. And just as you cross the orchard, there ... there lies Karbala. A high wall runs all around it. And enclosed within are the deserted grounds of Karbala. In one corner are two deep pits. The taazias belonging to the Shias are buried in one pit, in the other those belonging to the Sunnis. And the doorway ... how tall and grand it looks. An iron-barred gate, and on either side, two massive pillars and, sitting atop the pillars, two spires which have become black under the onslaught of sun and wind, and begun to look as though they are made of iron and have rusted over. The gate was opened only during Muharram; for the rest of the year, a massive lock dangled from it. When we used to peer through its barred gate at that sun-scorched barren wilderness, it truly looked like the desolate battleground of Karbala. And the searing loo that blasted us like a furnace seemed to come straight from the real Karbala.

On this side of the gate, next to the platform, stood Bholu's hut, and inside its unpaved courtyard a pitcher of water under a kaithu tree. We would take the water from a coconut shell tied to its mouth with a bit of twine, pour it into our mouths from a distance and, with our thirst slaked, sit down on the platform beside Bholu's hut. An exceptionally dense and old peepal tree grew in the middle of the platform, and so you could always find shade under it. The other trees, such as tamarind, grew along the left side of the Karbala wall. Those trees too were tall and dense. The tamarind fell from them in such abundance that you could never pick up all the fallen fruit. You could pick tamarind all the way from the Karbala wall until the elephant's grave. There was only one blood-red tamarind tree – the one that grew right beside the elephant's grave. If you bit into it, you could actually feel your mouth go red with its crimson juice.

Didn't I tell you – once I venture towards Karbala, I can never return. The place is such. But I can say no more about it, because I have not seen it for the past fifty years. I have never been able to reach it. The furthest I am able to go is till Babwa's wrestling pit. Even that makes me happy; my Karbala lies just beyond. All I need to do is enter the Sambhali's orchard, come out at the other end and I would have reached Karbala. But at that very moment, sleep deserts me and I wake up. Though, on one occasion, I even made it till Sambhali's grove. How fragrant was the grave of Sheikh Madad Ali Sambhali! The haarsingaar tree at its head had shed so many sweet-smelling flowers that the grave looked like a bed of haarsingaar blossoms. The dear departed Sheikh Sambhali used to recite the soz so soulfully that even the most stony-hearted would leave the majlis with drenched handkerchiefs. A dirge-like atmosphere prevailed in his Imambara on the eve of the eighth day of Muharram. The majlis for the big alam would begin after midnight and Sheikh Sahab would start the recitation in a voice wracked with pain:

'When Husain turned towards the canal...'

People would begin to sob from the first line and, by the time the alam was taken out, the beating of breasts would have started in earnest. The cymbals beating outside, the rising tempo of loud mourning inside – the very walls of the Imambara seemed to reverberate. Head spinning, dazed by grief, mourners would begin to fall to the ground like ninepins, from where they would be picked up by watchful attendants who would lug them outside, place them on settees and sprinkle so much rosewater to revive them that their face, neck and chest would become redolent and wet. The moment the call for the fajir prayer was heard, the cymbals would fall silent after one final resonant clap. The mourners would end the mourning and the alam with its shining, resplendent panja and the streamers speckled with red stains would be stored out of sight in the little room. That served as a signal for the sonorous lamentation to be reduced to muffled sobbing and the occasional hiccup. Soon after, sheer maal would be distributed. I would return home in the pearly twilight, clutching my portion of sheer maal. It would be nearly morning by the time I reached home.

History, too, has its moments of twilight. That year, Muharram fell on one such occasion. It was the last Muharram for Sheikh Madad Ali Sambhali. The son had already announced his intentions of leaving. The family would leave immediately after Muharram. As always, Sheikh sahab began reciting the soz on the eve of Muharram:

'On the night of departure, Shabbir went to the grave...'

But he was so overwhelmed by the first line itself that he never made it to the next. His sons had to take over and

complete the rest of the marsiya. Then, on the night of the
eighth day at the majlis for the big alam, the soz that was
traditionally narrated by Sheikh sahab had to be recited by
his sons. Sheikh sahab took to his bed and never got up again.
Within weeks, he was gone. The Sambhali family buried their
elder in the bosom of this land and went away forever.

Look how far I have digressed! As I was saying, on
that one occasion, I had made it till the Sambhali family's
orchard. Before that, I would be loitering in some alley
somewhere near Qayyuma's shop when I would rouse. Once,
something terrible happened. I lost my way. I would come
out of one alley and immediately find myself in another. Out
of the second, I would enter a third. Allah, save me from this
entrapment! What a web of alleys and back streets! My town
didn't have so many streets. Have I, then, come to some
other town? But no, it looks like my town. But where have all
these streets sprung from? Arre, have I somehow come out
in Qazi Khel? If this is Qazi Khel, where is Shavilat? I look
everywhere, but I cannot find Shavilat. No, then this can't
be Qazi Khel. It must be Hinduwada, then. Hinduwada had
extremely narrow streets, but every house had the figure of
Lord Hanuman painted with geru on the whitewashed wall
beside the front door. A little ahead you came to a chowk
with a well, whose parapet was made of red stone, right in
the middle of the crossroad. A few more steps and the alley
came to an end. Then you could go towards the road that
led to the open-air market. There, right ahead, you could
see the pond. If you don't see all this, this isn't Hinduwada. I
wandered around for a long time, worried that I must reach

Karbala. How long will I loiter in these streets? I walk a few steps and the road comes to an end. What is this? Have I walked into a dead end? A dead end? But there was no dead end in our mohalla. I fret for a long time: how could I have reached this dead end? How will I come out? How will I reach Karbala? But what do I see ... the dead end has disappeared. Instead, there is a flat expanse of ground. Empty and desolate. Not a living soul around. Ya Allah, where am I? What is this place? I spot a rustic-looking person walking past, carrying a bundle of grass on his head. I hurry to ask him, 'Where is the holy Karbala?'

'Karbala? Oh, you mean where the Musslas go with their tazias?'

'Yes, yes, that's the place.'

'Ask a Mussla. This is Ravan's Papdi.'

Ravan's Papdi? But there used to be a tall tamarind tree over there. Where has it gone? On those scorching afternoons, when we used to come this way, we would go only till the dharamshala. We would gaze at Ravan's Papdi from a distance; it was a desolate, eerie place. Not a blade of grass or bush or scrub grew on it. And only one tree. It stood bang in the middle of the field, looking like Ravan himself. As I was saying ... My heart began to beat furiously. I wanted to turn away immediately. Arre ... I have come to Qayyuma's shop. I have found my way. Instead of going straight ahead from here, if I turn left I will first come to the lane of the Ghosis, then the ruined tomb, then the old fort beside the hillock ... Arre, but where did the lane of the Ghosis go? Has it got lost? I am surprised. And then I awaken.

Once again, I have reached there. Once again, I am surprised. This used to be the ikka stand. And here was Ismail the shoemaker's shop. So many shoes displayed on shoe racks and a needle forever busy in his hand! Bits of shiny black and tan leather would be strewn all around him. Where has that shop gone? The snake charmer is playing his flute in front of a closed basket. A crowd of people, young and old, is standing in a circle around him. I too stand among them, as though I am a part of that crowd. Finally, the basket's lid falls open. Two hooded black snakes emerge and begin to sway. Their needle-sharp tongues dart in and out of their mouths. They are coming towards me and their hoods are becoming larger and larger. Suddenly my eyes fall on a grubby boy standing in front of me who has been staring at me instead of watching the snake show. Thoroughly rattled, I look around furtively and slip away from the crowd. I remember that I do not have a passport. I have been roaming around here without a passport. Fear grips me, and now I am all the more terrified of that boy who was staring at me. Has he recognized me? My heart begins to beat furiously. Did he see me slipping away? Is he following me? I quicken my step. I come out of one alley and quickly duck into another. From there, I enter a third. It is deserted. There isn't a soul around. Two jackals are standing beside the peepal tree and staring at me. My feet feel leaden, each weighing a hundred maund. Then my eyes open and I am awake. It is a good thing that I wake up. God knows what else awaited me! I have been saved. Because I had neither visa nor passport with me. I have only one claim over Guisetown, at least to my way of thinking I do. And it is that I am part of its soil. My umbilical cord is buried here. But what significance does that have? And even if you *are* part of that soil, so what? The thing that matters is the visa. Without a visa, a man who has left this land can never enter it, even in his dreams. So it was a good thing that I woke up when I did.

This is the only time that I have been relieved on waking up to find it was only a dream. Otherwise, I usually curse myself for waking up and wish that I could have slept some more. So that I could have dreamt some more, even if I had slept longer than the men who went to sleep in a cave and will be woken up on the Day of Judgment.[3] It is not as though I were trespassing; I was only wandering around the streets of my own town. Why couldn't I have wandered around some more? It felt good to be back on those streets. After all, it is only through these nocturnal wanderings in my dreams that I have come to know my city so well. When I lived there and used to see it all with my eyes wide open, it was tantamount to not knowing my own town! How much do any of us see with our waking eyes? Things reveal their true self only in dreams. That is why I was saying that the story called 'Qayyuma's Shop', that someone else wrote, has been thirsting for completion. I must write that story. And I

---

[3] The story of the men who went to sleep in a cave has been narrated in the Surah al Kahaf (Surah 18, verse 22) in the Holy Quran; a similar story is narrated in the Bible but there the number of sleepers is specified as seven and the incident is commonly referred to as the 'seven sleepers of Ephesus'.

must write it now, now that I have scoured that town in my dreams for fifty long years.

Fifty years is not an inconsiderable period. I mean the dreams of fifty long years. There are so many dreams that it is difficult to count them. Except for that one dream when I did not have a passport, every dream has been such that I have wished I could go on dreaming it forever. I have always regretted waking up because wakefulness brings nothing but misery and wretchedness; sleep brings such release. Save for that once, I have always felt sad on waking up, and also happy, happy because one night's sleep has given me so much, almost as though my lap has been filled with bounty. And sad because so much has been held back from me, almost as though it was within my grasp yet eluding me.

One morning, I felt particularly wretched on getting up. That was the night I had seen Bela. I felt as though I had gone back home. It had been left wide open. And empty. Arre, there is no one here. Where has everyone gone? I climb the stairs to the room upstairs. I open the window that looks out on the back street, and there, across the street, is Lala Pyare Lal's tall house. I open the window … and what do I see? There, in front of me stands Bela on the roof of her house, drying her hair. She looks so pretty. Bela was never this pretty. She looks like a fairy who has flown down from Fairyland and landed on Lala Pyare Lal's roof. I feel like jumping across to her roof and touching her to see if she is real, is she really Bela?

I keep looking at her like a moron. Then I go close to her and say, 'Bela? You are Bela, aren't you?'

'No, I am Beecha.' She gives a peal of laughter, then turns around and slams the door shut. She slammed the door so hard that its deafening sound woke me up.

I never saw her again. How I longed to see her in my dreams again! But dreams come of their own volition. And they come suddenly, unexpectedly.

After that, I thought of Bela on many occasions, but always with regret: why did I never see how pretty she was in those days? Why did I always make awful faces at her? Whenever I would spot her on her roof, I would start making hideous faces at her and she would call out to her mother, 'Ma, look, that Mussla is making faces at me again.' I would immediately duck behind the window.

Once, on the occasion of Holi, a troupe of dancers and singers had come from the nearby villages. I spotted Bela, standing in the crowd and watching the Holi revellers beating their drums and singing and dancing. I went and stood close beside her. She was so engrossed in watching the dancers that she didn't even know. This was the first time I had had the opportunity to stand so close to her. I said to her, very sweetly, 'Bela.' She turned around with a start, saw me, hissed, 'Get lost, you Mussla!' and was gone.

Then, there was a dream that made me laugh, and also saddened me. We are leaving Guisetown. As we are about to turn the corner, my eyes fall on the roof of our house. How black it has become under the onslaught of wind and rain and also how dilapidated! A kite comes and lands on its parapet. A paper kite, with its torn string dangling behind it, swims in a lazy current of air. Its crimson string skims the parapet as it floats past. My heart begins to sink. The ikka turns the corner and, within a single beat of my heart, the blackened, tumbledown parapet of my house disappears from my sight.

I laugh. What a dream! It was only the sooty, moss-encrusted, half-broken parapet of our old house, not the arch of the Alhambra Mosque! And it is not as though I am leaving Cordova behind me! It was only Guisetown. One may well sigh when one is leaving something precious behind, not when one is leaving something as commonplace as Guisetown which could never make a place for itself in history. How I laughed! Then I sobered down and that sooty, moss-encrusted, half-broken parapet swam before my eyes for a long, long time. And then it occurred to me: had I actually left that place, or was I still there, left behind? After a very long time, I feel like laughing. After so many dreams, that moss-encrusted, broken-down parapet has finally revealed itself to me! Once again, sadness overwhelms me. Swimming before my eyes are all those kites whose strings others had cut and I had grabbed while standing on that parapet. And also those other kites which had eluded my grasping fingers and outstretched hands, and simply floated past. And also all those other kites with long dangling strings that must have skimmed past my parapet. Someone else must have grabbed them. A kite whose string has been cut is bound to be grabbed by someone or the other. Such is the fate of a kite whose string has been cut by another kite. There are very few kites that manage to elude the grasping fingers and outstretched hands of eagle-eyed little boys, and find a safe haven in the tangled branches of tall trees.

Anyhow, I am not about to write an epic on the rise and fall of kites. Such a story would be long and also quite heart-rending. Neither do I intend to write the history of my fifty-year-old dreams. I can't, in any case, write that since I do not remember any of my dreams in their entirety. Every dream rises before me in my subconscious as though there is a great deal preceding it that I have already seen and whatever I am now seeing is actually only a dream, and I am slipping, slipping through the circle of sense and sensibility. And then the dream ends, or rather doesn't end; it simply dissolves. In any case, a dream is not a short story or novel that it ought to have a plot with a well-defined beginning, middle and end. Even so, my dreams are unusually unconnected, unrelated. I mean the dreams I have dreamt in these past fifty years. Or so I think. It is almost as though every dream is a link in a long chain. Yet all my dreams are so separate, so unrelated. That story about Qayyuma's shop that I have been wanting to write again ... suppose that turns out to be equally unconnected? My story is not like a proper story; it is like the telling of a dream. Actually, it is so pitiable that a real, living city should be reduced to a dream. Guisetown existed fifty years ago, and fifty years later it is still there. If anything, it is more real. Because in these fifty years, the towns and cities of this subcontinent have made great progress in terms of trade and commerce. Great new plazas, shopping malls, housing colonies, apartment blocks and bungalows have mushroomed. Guisetown, too, has grown in proportion to my imaginary contretemps. That is, it is no longer the Guisetown of Qayyuma's time. Now this town has grown and spread so much that it is difficult to describe it within the framework of a short story or novel. Be that as it may, I still have to rewrite that story – whether fully or partially. As the writer has said, while writing 'Qayyuma's Shop', he forgot to describe the real character of his story. All the characters described in that story were minor characters. Qayyuma himself was a minor character. The day he closed his shop and left Guisetown, he became a minor character.

The protagonist of the story is the person who stayed behind. At that time, it did not occur to any of us that he was not leaving with us. He was rooted in that land; he did not budge when the rest of us were leaving. The writer did not think of him even when he was writing his story; he simply went on describing Qayyuma. It was only later that it occurred to us that that person who was one of us was no longer with us. Where is he now? He used to sit on the stoop of Qayyuma's shop. And now that Qayyuma's shop is closed, where is he? Has he found a new perch? No one seems to know his whereabouts.

I have come to know every little detail about my town through my dreams. And it is so strange that he has never appeared in any of my dreams. He is the only one who has never appeared in my dreams. Except for him, there is no one from Guisetown who has not, at some time or the other, come in my dreams. Even Bela has come in my dream on one memorable occasion and shown me a tantalizing glimpse of herself. What a glimpse that was! There she was drying her hair! Such long hair! Fairies are said to have such beautiful long hair. And what a lovely, full bosom! I must have been blind when I lived there. I was so busy making faces at her that I never saw the beauty she was. Anyhow, had I seen her beauty, this story would have become Bela's. So it was a good thing that I never saw her for what she was. But why has that person never appeared in my dreams?

I have suffered defeat in my dreams on only two counts. One, I have never ever been able to reach Karbala in any of my dreams. And, second, I have never been able to find that person in my dreams. For fifty years, I have been wandering in this dreamscape. Are these my dreams or the Fourth Corner of the world? Once, a world-weary all-knowing king said to his son: 'Conquering the world has been the glorious tradition of all great rulers. So go out and conquer the world.' At the same time, the old father, who had seen the ups and downs of life, cautioned his son, 'Go to the Three Corners of the world, but do not ever step into the Fourth Corner for here lies endless hardship for the conquerors of this world.' The young prince heeded his father's sage counsel. But once, while chasing a deer, he unwittingly entered the Fourth Corner. The deer soon disappeared and the bewildered prince found himself alone in the terrifying lifeless jungle.

My dreams are my terrifying lifeless jungle. I have been wandering alone in this jungle for so long. But my destination is as far away as it has always been in my dreams. I can see the spires of Karbala and I am on my way there when the thread of my dream snaps. And that lost person ... what about him? There has never been any news of him.

Aah ko chahiye ek umr asar hone tak
(It needs an age to make a sigh come true.)

But an age has passed. Fifty years *are* an age. Now I shall ask He who grants life to grant me another life. Karbala is still so far away. When will I find the person who has been lost? When will I see that one dream, the hope of which has been sustaining me all along? When will that dream be united with my wakeful self? When will I write my story? Or will I forever circle round and round in a gyre?

Sleep[1]

Zafar was amazed at the sight of him. 'Arre, Salman! You? You have come back? But how?'

'Don't ask how. I've come back. That is all.'

Zafar didn't know what to say next. 'To come back alive from there ... it's a miracle!'

'Yes, consider it a miracle. I was meant to live longer, so I have returned.'

It wasn't just Zafar who was amazed at his return; Salman himself could barely believe it. 'I can't believe that I have come away from that place.'

Zafar couldn't take his eyes off Salman. Salman was the only person he knew who had come back alive from there. He looked at Salman from head to toe and asked incredulously, 'But, tell me, Salman, how *did* you escape?'

'How did I escape,' he mumbled. For a moment he felt like spewing out his entire tale in one breath. He looked around, then said, 'I can't tell you in a few words; it requires

---

[1] Published as 'Neend' in the short story collection *Kachhuwe* (*Tortoises*), Sang-e-Meel Publications, Lahore, 1995.

a marathon storytelling session. You will lose your senses if you hear the details.'

'You are right, my friend. The little that we have heard is horrifying, whereas you – you have seen it all with your own eyes.'

He drew a long breath and sighed. 'Yes, yes, I have seen it all with my own eyes.'

Countless macabre scenes danced before his eyes. 'I have seen so much that ... Let's just say I have seen it all.'

'Tell me.'

Once again, Salman wanted to spit it all out, but he looked around and checked himself. 'I have a lot to tell you, but how can I ... standing here like this?'

Zafar paused to think, then asked, 'What are you doing in the evening?'

'Morning or evening, nothing matters to me ... they are the same.'

'Then come home this evening.'

'All right, I'll be there.'

'I'll call Aslam. He'll come too.'

'Aslam the Argumentative. Is he still around?'

'Nothing ever happens to people like him; they are spared both living and dying. Where will he go?'

'What about Zaidi?'

'I'll call that big-talker too. So, are we fixed for the evening?'

'Yes, we are.'

Zafar reached home and quickly dialled a number. 'Hello? Aslam? Yaar, it's me ... Zafar. Yaar, Salman has returned.'

'Salman? What are you saying, yaar!'

'Yes, yes. He has returned.'

'You mean, he has escaped from there? Alive? But how?'

'Come home this evening and ask him yourself.'

'I'll be there.'

Then he called Zaidi at his office. 'Hello, Zaidi ... Please call Zaidi ... Hello, Zaidi? It's me, Zafar. Can I tell you something?'

'Tell me.'

'Salman has come back.'

'Salman! No way, man!'

'Yes, he managed to get away.'

'What a thick-skinned bloke! Where is he now?'

'Come home this evening. He'll be there.'

'I'll come.'

All four friends met in the evening. The three looked at Salman in utter amazement and Salman looked at them, equally bemused. Aslam expressed their collective astonishment at his escape, then spoke of his sorrow at the state of affairs there. As he spoke, his anger grew. 'How they have tortured people over there ... They have killed and maimed the old ... children ... women ... barbarians ... animals ... If I had my way, I would ...' He gritted his teeth.

'They should have done precisely this,' Zaidi announced.

'Done this?' Aslam spluttered in angry disbelief.

'After what we have been doing to them for twenty-five years, this is precisely what they should have done,' Zaidi said.

'And what have we been doing? What did we do to them?' Aslam shouted.

Then he launched into a long tirade on all the atrocities committed by them, his knowledge gleaned from several sensational newspaper reports. Zaidi countered each of the allegations and, in turn, listed all the cruelties they had been perpetrating against them. Salman yawned. Zafar looked at him and asked, 'What do you think, Salman?'

Aslam pounced, 'Yes, let's ask Salman. He has lived there for so many years. He has seen everything with his own eyes. What do you think, Salman?'

'I think …' Salman said and fell into a contemplative silence.

Zafar became impatient. He prodded, 'Yes, come on, tell us. Say something.'

'What shall I say?'

Zaidi sneered, 'Scared of commitment?'

'Commitment?' Salman gaped uncomprehendingly.

Aslam spoke forcefully, 'Let's hear what you have to say about the situation there.'

Somewhat uncertainly, Salman said, 'Yaar, I don't know what to make of it.'

Zafar looked daggers at him. 'The last time you were here, you had picked my brains clean going on and on about that place.'

Salman simply gazed at Zafar, then spoke in a muffled voice, 'At the time I thought that I understood the situation.'

'Forget all that. Tell us what happened there.'

'Yes, that I can tell you,' he spoke with complete conviction. 'I have seen a great deal there. If I begin to describe all that I have seen, you will break out in goose pimples,' he said, then fell silent as though he were preparing to launch into an epic. The three friends sat in rapt attention. They waited for him to continue. But he just sat there. When he didn't utter another word, Zafar prompted, 'Yaar, you haven't told us anything yet.'

'Yes, yaar,' he fumbled, 'Yaar, I don't know what to say. I can't remember anything.'

Both Aslam and Zaidi glared at him, then turned away and started talking among themselves as though they didn't know him.

They talked and argued and squabbled among themselves. Things began to warm up. Tempers rose. Volleys of sarcasm jetted back and forth. Resounding abuse burst from Zafar, sometimes about people on that side, sometimes about those on this side. Salman looked at one friend, then the other. He listened without saying a word. His eyelids began to droop. Once or twice, he nearly dozed off. Then he pulled himself up and tried to listen attentively to every contentious word that was being said. Again, his lids grew heavy and his eyes began to close.

'Bastards! Democratic dogs!' Zaidi banged the table with his fist.

'Bunch of bloody traitors! They are all Indian agents!' Aslam hissed. Salman looked at them with drowsy eyes and drifted back to sleep.

He opened his eyes when tea was placed before them and Zafar nudged him, 'Salman, here's your tea.' He woke up with a start, looked apologetically at his friends and sat up straight. Softly, he ran his fingers over his eyes, then took a sip of tea. As he drank the tea, he could feel the sleep leaving his eyes. Now he felt refreshed as though the doors and windows of his mind were opening. He said, 'The way I dozed off just now reminds me of an incident from those days. That night I hadn't slept a wink.' As he spoke, countless terrifying visions began to dance before his eyes and a subhuman scream ricocheted through his brain.

'Which night are you talking about? Was it before the fall?' Aslam asked.[2]

Salman thought for a moment, then said, 'I can't remember which night it was, but those nights were all the same, except that ...' and he fell silent. Aslam, Zaidi and Zafar had been listening closely. Disconcerted by their attention, Salman skittered, 'I forgot what I was about to say. Anyhow, after that, I wasn't able to sleep all night.' He paused, then said, 'And after that, sleep became a rarity. Perhaps, I haven't slept at all ever since. Or, maybe, I have on one or two occasions ...' Aslam, Zaidi and Zafar listened listlessly. Then they became engrossed in their own conversation. Back and forth the arguments raged – did people from the other side exploit them or did our own people betray us? Salman just sat there, trying to recollect whether he had slept at all during any of the endless nights. He couldn't remember. And what about since he had come here? He couldn't remember that either.

Tired of his futile calculations, he tried to concentrate on the argument raging between Zafar, Zaidi and Aslam.

---

[2] The Fall of Dhaka refers to the surrender by the West Pakistan army on 16 December 1971.

He kept listening, until a yawn caught him unawares and he looked at Zafar with sleep-drowned eyes, and said, 'Yaar, I am feeling sleepy.'

Zafar gave him an insipid look and said, 'So why don't you sleep?'

'Yes, I am going to sleep,' he said in a muffled, somnolent voice as his eyes began to close. He slipped down the sofa, rested his head on the headrest and put his feet up on the table. With one worn slipper resting near Aslam and the toe of the other nudging Zaidi, he began to snore.

Captive[1]

'So … tell me how things are out here.'

'Here? What can I tell you about things here?'

The question was actually quite unexpected for Anwar. Perhaps not consciously, perhaps unconsciously, he had already made up his mind that whatever will be, will be. He was probing about things out there, yet when he was asked about the state of affairs here, he was caught off guard.

'What happened here?' Javed asked again.

'Here?' he repeated wonderingly and got lost in thought. Finally, he said, 'Yaar, but nothing happened here.'

'Nothing?'

'Honestly! Nothing happened. Compared to what you saw there, nothing happened here.'

'Really! There we were thinking that a lot must have happened here as well.'

'Yes, yaar, nothing happened here, nothing at all.' There was shame and sorrow in Anwar's tone.

---

[1] Published as 'Aseer' in the short story collection *Kachhuwe (Tortoises)*, Sang-e-Meel Publications, Lahore, 1995.

'But there was a war here, too, wasn't there?'

'Yes, the war happened,' Anwar's voice was subdued. The conversation ground to a standstill. The enthusiasm with which Anwar had begun his questions had cooled off. Javed had made an idle query. There wasn't sufficient curiosity and eagerness behind his questions.

Anwar spoke up again. 'Actually, there were no outside forces at work here. Whatever happened was wrought from within.'

'Nothing ever happens because of factors outside,' Javed said in all earnestness. 'Whatever happens, happens from inside.'

'No, not always,' Anwar said with some heat. 'Most of what happened there, happened from outside. Whereas, here, whatever happened was a purely internal matter. That is why most of it happened after the war.'

'Really?'

'Yes.'

'But what exactly happened?'

'Strikes, lockouts, marches, protests, street fights, students' unrest, arrests ...'

Javed picked up an illustrated magazine from the table in front of them and began to turn its pages. The magazine had been lying on the table since the morning, but either he had not had the time to look at it, or he hadn't felt like reading it. But now, the magazine pulled him towards itself irresistibly. He loved the photographs in it.

'Something like a domestic war broke out in the university. Barricades were put up, sten guns were brought in and the sound of bullets could be heard all night.'

'That's good.' Javed smiled.

'What?'

'This cartoon, here…' Javed turned the magazine towards Anwar.

Anwar glanced at the cartoon moodily and muttered, 'It's nice,' and lapsed into silence.

'Let's go out,' Javed suggested.

'All right.'

'We will talk in circles all night if we stay at home. There will be a constant stream of visitors; everyone has the same questions and the same answers. It is the new definition of captivity. Let's go, yaar.' He jumped to his feet, walked towards the inner door and called in a loud voice, 'I am going out with Anwar.' And the two stepped out.

'Yaar, did you hear about the riots in Sindh?' Anwar suddenly remembered how damaging and tragic the crisis had been. It was important to inform Javed of it.

'You couldn't have learnt much from the radio bulletins. Some truly amazing things have been happening here. Scores of people died, so many became homeless. You must have seen Liaqat Market. It was such a huge market. It was razed to the ground; not a soul escaped alive …'

'Yaar, what are these squares on the stomach and thighs?' Javed asked and stopped in his tracks.

Anwar stopped mid-sentence and looked in the direction in which Javed was staring, transfixed. There was a poster hanging in front of the cinema hall showing a half-naked woman. A grid of squares was drawn on her well-rounded thighs and stomach. This poster that Anwar was wont to gaze at with some diligence every time he passed it now offended him greatly. 'Forget it, yaar,' he said and the two walked on.

'Will you have an ice-cream?' Anwar stopped in front of a shop.

'Okay.'

While eating his ice-cream, Javed's eyes fell upon a girl who was wearing flappers and huge round goggles. He continued to inspect her minutely till she left the shop.

'Yaar, Anwar, the bell-bottom seems to have disappeared during my absence.'

'And tight pants too.'

'Yes, tight pants and tight shirts too ... Yaar, you still haven't told me what happened here.'

'You can see what happened here,' Anwar said slyly, eating his ice-cream. 'The bell-bottom has gone and the flapper has come in.'

'This is no small matter,' Javed said.

'No, it is a huge, huge matter.' Anwar's tone was loaded with sarcasm. He stopped, then asked, 'So, what are your views on this huge matter?'

'Yaar, I have not quite been able to reconcile myself to this flapper business.' He finished his ice-cream and dumped the empty cup in a trash bin. 'Shall we go?'

'Yes, let's go.'

They walked on.

Anwar was no longer in a serious mood. But seeing Javed's curiosity regarding several small, insignificant matters, he couldn't resist asking, 'Now that you are here, what is your reaction?'

'Reaction? My reaction? What do you mean?'

'I mean, after your long years in captivity, now that you are here, what do you feel?'

'You know, it is strange…' Javed stopped in his tracks again.

'What happened?'

'Look at that young man… he is wearing a pink salwar and, if I am not mistaken, it is silken.'

'So what?'

'You mean nothing is wrong? Really?' Javed fell silent for a while, then said, 'Do the youth favour such colours and fabrics nowadays? I have seen other young people wearing bright colours and silken salwar-kurtas.'

'Yes, it is quite common these days. Listen, do you want to eat kadhai gosht?'

'Kadhai gosht?'

'Yes, yes, it is almost dinner-time. Why go home? Let's eat kadhai gosht and then go for a long walk.'

It was crowded. Cars were parked on both sides of the road. Tables and chairs were laid out on the lawn and the footpath. All the tables were taken. Beneath a gigantic picture of a goat, rows upon rows of entire roasted legs of mutton were strung. The ovens were roaring, hissing and spitting sparks.

'Yaar, the place is so crowded.'

'Don't worry; we'll get a table soon,' Anwar said and spied a far-off table emptying. He pounced on it. The table was on the footpath. A car was parked nearby. The bonnet of another car parked close beside it was being used as a tabletop. Balanced on it were a couple of kadhais laden with meat and bent over them a few girls and boys. 'Yaar, this too must have happened after I left.' Javed looked around at the other diners.

'What?'

'This business of kadhai gosht.'

'Yes, this is the newest dish in town.'

Javed looked around once again. He took in the rows of cars, the tables, the chairs, the diners ... 'Yaar, this used to be a very quiet part of town.' He stopped, then added, 'And the strange thing is that everyone is eating tikka kababs and kadhai gosht. There weren't so many shops selling tikka kababs, were there?'

Anwar was clearly not listening. His eyes were fixed on the tandoors. 'It has been so long; our food still hasn't come.'

Javed looked around lingeringly. Young and old, male and female, delicate young girls, pot-bellied men – everyone was engrossed in eating. At a table nearby, a robust-looking individual, drenched in sweat, was attacking his food with a single-minded ferocity. At another table sat a suited-booted man and a nubile young woman daintily wrapped in a sari, with an empty kadhai between them. There was a heap of chewed bones on the lady's plate and she herself was sucking heartily at a bone. All around there were tables laden with meat-filled kadhais and giant-sized bites entering gaping maws, and everywhere there was the clamping of jaws, munching, chewing and chomping. Javed could imagine the jaws becoming bigger and bigger. His surprise was fast turning into horror.

'Yaar, Anwar,' he said in a worried voice, 'people have started eating rather a lot now.'

Anwar barely heard him. The kadhai had reached their table. 'Come on, let's dig in.'

Javed put a morsel in his mouth and thought, 'My jaws are gigantic.'

'You are not eating, yaar!'

'I am, I am.'

'No you are not. It won't do being polite here. This is kadhai gosht; it must be eaten caveman-style.'

He took several large bites to please Anwar, but soon he slowed down. His thoughts began to wander. 'Yaar, how is Khalid? I still haven't met any of the others.'

'Khalid?' Anwar's hand stopped in mid-air where he was reaching for another giant-sized bite. 'Didn't I tell you about Khalid?'

'No, you didn't.'

Anwar swallowed, then spoke softly, 'Yaar, Khalid is no more.'

'Really … him too?' He was lost in thought. 'Yaar, you have been telling me of the passing away of so many of our friends. So many people have died in these two years!'

'People have died very quickly in these two years.'

'And everyone has died in their beds,' Javed spoke in a tone of mild wonderment.

'What? What do you mean?' Anwar was shocked.

'Out there, people die differently. We didn't know about their traditional way of dying.' He paused, then continued, 'That is why we found Rasheed's death so odd.'

'Rasheed? He's dead? Didn't he live in Rajshahi?'

'Yes, he did, but towards the end he had fled Rajshahi and come to live in Dhaka. He stayed with me for a few days … then he died … lay down on the bed and died.'

'So, Rasheed too is dead,' Anwar muttered, half to himself, in sorrow.

'Yes, we gave him a proper shroud and a decent burial.'

Anwar looked askance. What a strange thing to say!

'Rasheed's death was probably the last traditional death in that country,' Javed said, by way of explaining his earlier comments. Then he fell silent.

For some time, both sat in silence. They ate a little, toyed with the food, drank some water and sat back. Javed glanced around once again. The faces had changed. There were fresh kadhais on several tables and new diners with new jaws working in the same untiring way. The jaws were getting bigger and bigger. He turned his eyes away and said, 'You were asking about my feelings and reactions since I came back, weren't you?'

'Yes.'

'Yaar, at first I felt as though everything had changed here, everything. I felt jolted, almost disoriented. Gradually, I began to see that nothing had changed here; again I felt disoriented.'

'What is the connection between these two feelings?' Anwar asked in amazement.

'There is no connection at all. Well, never mind, let it be,' Javed said, swiftly changing the subject. 'Tell me about the situation here.'

'There is nothing to tell.' By now Anwar was so thoroughly dispirited that he did not have the heart for any more stories.

'So, whom were you talking about yesterday?'

'Was I? I don't remember.'

'The one who was shot?'

'Oh! You mean Mirza ...'

'Mirza was killed by a bullet? Who shot him?'

'He was leaving a demonstration. The street was crowded.'

'That is the problem with demonstrations; streets become clogged. What happened then?'

'He crossed the street ... he must have taken barely four steps when someone fired a gun and he died instantly.'

'But who fired the gun and why?'

'Someone must have ... just like that.'

'Strange, very strange, indeed! Then what happened?'

'That's it.'

'You mean nothing happened after that?' There was terror in his voice now.

'No, nothing. What could happen after that?'

'A man is killed by a bullet, and nothing happens. That is strange, isn't it Anwar?'

'Perhaps you are right. I hadn't ever thought of it before. '

'You never thought of it?' He looked at Anwar with a mix of surprise and fear.

'Yes, yaar,' he said with something approaching shame and began to look at Javed with some perplexity.

'Javed!'

'Yes! What is it?'

'Yaar.' A little scared now, he tried to probe one last time. 'You must have seen worse things out there … hmm?'

Javed hesitated. 'Yes,' he said sorrowfully, 'you are right. But at least we knew why it was happening to us … at least we understood what was happening.'

Those Who Are Lost[1]

The man rested his wounded head against the tree trunk, opened his eyes and asked, 'Have we come out?'

The bearded man answered in a tone of quiet contentment, 'Praise be to the Lord, we have emerged unscathed.'

The man with a bag slung around his neck nodded in agreement. 'Yes, undoubtedly, we have managed to save our lives and get away.' Then he looked at the bandage tied around the head of the injured man and asked, 'How's your head now?'

The man replied, 'I think some blood is still seeping from it.'

The bearded man spoke in the same tone of quiet contentment, 'Don't worry, my friend. The bleeding will stop and, if the Good Lord so wills, the wound will soon heal.'

The man with the wounded head now opened his eyes fully and looked at each of them closely. Then he lifted a finger and counted them – the bearded man, the man with

---

[1] Published as 'Woh Jo Kho Gaye' in *Intizar Husain aur Unke Afsane,* Educational Book House, Aligarh.

the bag slung around his neck and the youth. Surprised, he asked, 'Where is the other man?'

The youth was startled. 'Who? You mean ... one of us is missing?'

The bearded man glared at the youth. Then he spoke to the man with the wounded head in a soft, chiding tone, 'My friend, our numbers are not so large that we can go wrong in counting.'

The man with the bag agreed with the bearded man, then he too counted each of them – the bearded man, the man with the wounded head and the youth. He too was startled, 'Where is the other man?'

The youth looked despairingly at the man with the bag. Then he counted them all over again – the bearded man, the man with the bag and the man with the wounded head. Sounding quite worried, he asked, 'Where has the other man gone?'

The bearded man looked at the trio with stabbing, angry eyes. He raised a finger and took in each of the three – the man with the wounded head, the man with the bag and the youth. It was his turn to be startled. He counted them again. Again he was startled. He counted them for the third time, slowly and carefully. Rattled, he muttered, 'Strange, very strange!'

The foursome looked at each other in fearful bewilderment. And the same exclamation rose in whispered unison to their lips, 'Strange, very strange, indeed!' And then they fell silent.

It was a long silence. A dog started barking somewhere in the distance. The youth looked at the others with fear-filled eyes and said softly, 'Why is the dog barking?'

The man with the wounded head was indifferent to his question. 'Who can it be?'

'Must be him,' the bearded man spoke confidently in a loud, ringing tone. 'He can't be very far away; he must have gotten lost somewhere close by.'

The man with the wounded head picked up a bamboo staff and got to his feet. 'If it is him, and the dog is stopping him from getting here, I must go and fetch him.'

He held the bamboo staff and began to walk in the direction of the barking dog. The remaining three sat in silence. The man with the bag asked, 'Can it really be him?'

The bearded man said, 'Who else can it be at this strange hour in this strange land?'

'Yes, it must be him,' the man with the bag spoke complacently. 'He was always so scared of dogs. If ever he spotted a dog on the road, he would become still as a statue.'

But the youth spoke doubtingly, 'Have you noticed ... the sound of the barking can't be heard any more.'

The man with the bag tried to listen closely, then said, 'Yes, that's true, there is no sound now. I wonder what could have happened.'

The bearded man spoke reassuringly, 'The two of them must have chased the dog away. They will be here any moment now.'

And the three fell silent again. Their eyes had turned in the direction the man with the wounded head had taken. The man with the bag was staring unblinkingly. He spoke as though he had suddenly spotted something, 'He is coming alone.'

'Alone?' the bearded man asked.

'Yes, alone.'

The three watched the man with the wounded head as he came closer. The man with the wounded head came up to them, put his staff away and sat down. He said, 'There was no one there.'

The man with the bag asked incredulously, 'But then, why did the dog bark?'

The youth said, 'Dogs don't bark just like that.'

The man with the wounded head said, 'But there was no one there.'

'That's very strange,' the man with the bag said.

The youth pricked his ears again. He said, 'Listen ... what do you make of that? Isn't it the sound of a barking dog?'

Everyone listened carefully. Then the bearded man said to the man with the wounded head, 'Where did you go off to? The sound of barking is coming from the other direction.'

The man with the bag picked up the bamboo staff lying close beside the man with the wounded head and got up. He said, 'I will go and see.'

The bearded man also got to his feet and said, 'Why don't we all go and see?'

The other two also got to their feet. All four of them set off in the direction from which they had just heard the barking. They walked very far. But they found nothing. The man with the bag muttered as he walked, 'There is no one here.'

The bearded man tried to bolster his courage. He said, 'Call out to him; he must be somewhere close by. He is a man, not a phantom that he will disappear like this.'

The man with the wounded head spoke despairingly, 'Yes, call out to him and see.' And he took a long shuddering breath as though he was plucking all his courage to call out but, suddenly, he stopped short. He turned towards the man with the bag and said, 'I can't remember his name. What was his name?'

'Name?'

The man with the wounded head tried hard to recall the missing man's name but to no avail. Then he turned towards the youth, 'Surely you must remember, young man.'

The youth replied, 'Forget the name, I don't even remember his face.'

'Don't even remember his face …' and the man with the bag fell into deep thought. Finally, he said, 'You know, it is amazing; even I cannot remember his face.' He turned towards the bearded man. 'Sir, surely you remember his face and his name.'

The bearded man was lost in thought. He tried hard to dredge it up from his memory. Then he spoke in a worried tone, 'Friends, let us turn back, for there is danger in searching any further.'

'Why?'

'Because we remember neither his name nor his face. In such a situation, God knows what we might chance upon. We might think it is he, and it might not be him but someone else. This is a strange hour and we are in a strange land.'

The four of them turned back. They walked till they reached the spot from which they had set off. They got a fire going and the man with the bag took out some mixed gram from the bag and began to cook it.

After they had eaten and drunk, they sat warming their hands by the fire. Remembering those they had left behind, they grew tearful.

'But who was that man?' the youth asked.

The others feigned ignorance and asked, 'Which man?'

'The man who was with us but got left behind.'

'Oh … that man … we had nearly forgotten him. Yes, who was he?'

'It is very strange,' said the man with the bag. 'We don't even remember his face or his name.'

'Wasn't he one of us, then?'

The youth's question left them dumbfounded. Then the man with the bag said, 'If he wasn't one of us, who was he? And why was he tagging along with us? His sudden disappearance …' He fell silent. They looked at each other as though each was trying to fathom why the man had disappeared, why he was with them, who, how, when …

Finally, the bearded man gathered their flailing courage and said, 'Friends, do not succumb to doubts, for doubts hold no recompense for us. He was undoubtedly one of us. But we left our homes in such disarray that we could not possibly recognize our fellow men, nor could we keep track of our numbers as we fled.'

'But why can't we remember how many of us there were when we left?' the youth interjected. 'And where we had left from …' he added.

The bearded man tried hard to remember. 'All I can remember is that when I left Gharnata ...'

'Left Gharnata ...' the three were startled and looked at the bearded man in amazement.

Then the man with the bag began to laugh loudly. The bearded man had stopped short at the others' amazement. Now he was thoroughly rattled by the laughter of the man with the bag. The man with the bag went on laughing and said, 'It is like, if I were to start boasting and say, "When I was leaving Jehanabad ..."'

Jehanabad? Everyone was shocked.

Now the man with the bag, who had been laughing at the bearded man all this while, was jolted into silence. The man with the wounded head gave a sharp, hard cackle of laughter and said a bit sorrowfully, 'I have been uprooted, so it does not matter any more whether I left Gharnata or Jehanabad or Mecca, the Most Sacred of Homes, or Kashmir ...' and he too fell silent.

These words of the man with the wounded head so affected them that they all fell silent. After a while, the bearded man spoke tearfully, 'We have left behind everything that we owned, but must we leave our memories as well?'

The man with the bag spoke after a great deal of thought, 'All I can remember now is that our homes were burning like dry kindling and we were running out and running away.'

The youth's heart grew heavy. He said, 'All I can remember is that at that moment, my father was sitting on his prayer mat holding a rosary in his hand. His lips were moving in prayer and there was smoke billowing all around us ...'

The bearded man asked in a soft, cloying tone, 'Did your father live to see all this?' The youth made no answer. His eyes were brimming with tears.

The man with the bag spoke pensively, 'All I can remember is that our homes were burning like piles of tinder and we were running out in blind panic.'

The man with the wounded head remained unperturbed. All he said was, 'Friends, what's the good of memories? How does it help me to remember whether my head was struck with a bamboo pole or a stick or whether it was cleaved in two by a sword? All that matters to me is that right now, at this very moment, my head is aching unbearably and blood is trickling down it.'

Everyone looked at the man with the wounded head with deep sympathy.

The bearded man looked long and lingeringly at the man with the wounded head and said, 'My breast has more wounds than your head.' He sighed deeply and continued, 'Oh, what a town it was before it was razed to the ground!'

'What a crowd of people and how quickly they disappeared before our eyes!' the youth spoke dolefully. He was lost in a maze of memories. He remembered the moment when he had placed his very first kiss on a pair of tremulous lips. He remembered making those grandiose announcements that one usually makes at such moments and how lowly time and place seem to become and how magical the path of love. Now he recalled the moment with sadness. He muttered, 'Had she been here now, our numbers would have been even.'

'She?' The bearded man looked askance. 'Had who been here?'

'Her.'

'Who?'

The youth made no reply. He was looking unblinkingly into empty space. The bearded man and the man with the bag continued to watch him. The man with the wounded head leaned back against the tree and closed his eyes as though he were heartily sick of this whole business. The man with the bag finally asked softly, 'Was it a woman?'

'Woman?' The bearded man jumped at the word.

The man with the wounded head also opened his eyes in surprise.

'If it was a woman,' the man with the bag said, 'God knows we have been deprived of good companionship!'

The bearded man looked daggers at him and said, 'If it was a woman, God knows, her companionship would have ruined us all!'

The man with the wounded head laughed sardonically and asked, 'Aren't we already ruined?'

'But that ruin would have been far worse.'

Then the man with the wounded head spoke in a suddenly cruel tone, 'You old man, it is far better to come to naught because of a woman than to have to suffer like this – without reason, without cause.' And he closed his eyes and rested his head once more against the tree trunk.

There was a long silence. The man with the bag got up to collect bits of firewood and stoke the fire. They continued to sit like that – each lost in his own thoughts, drowning in their own forebodings, warming their hands beside the fire – until finally the bearded man muttered, 'Isn't it strange that we can neither remember his name nor his face? We can't even remember whether this person was a man or a woman.'

The man with the bag spoke as though he was putting immense pressure on his brain to recall something. 'Who was the missing person? Who could it be?' And then he added suspiciously, 'What if it wasn't a man?'

'Not a man?' The youth was perplexed.

The bearded man hesitated then said softly, 'Yes, it could be so.'

Again, there was silence. The youth was caught in a snare. He asked, 'If it wasn't a man, who was it?'

The bearded man and the man with the bag fell into deep thought. The man with the wounded head opened his eyes, looked at the youth and said, 'If it wasn't a woman, who was she? And if she was a creature from hell, to hell with her!' And he closed his eyes once again.

'Creature from hell!' The other three were startled. After a moment's hesitation, the bearded man said, 'Friend, don't talk like that lest we lose trust in our fellow men.'

The man with the wounded head opened his eyes and looked at the bearded man. Once again he laughed in his typically sardonic manner and said, 'Old man, do you still repose trust in your fellow men?' He closed his eyes, put his head back and slumped against the tree trunk.

The bearded man looked worriedly at him and asked, 'Friend, does your head hurt a lot?'

The man with the wounded head kept his eyes closed, but shook his head in negation. He stayed quiet. The bearded man probed, 'Do you remember how you were hurt? And how you escaped?'

The man with the wounded head kept his eyes shut, but spoke in a tone of extreme torment, 'I don't remember anything.'

'How strange!' said the youth.

'No, there is nothing strange about it,' said the bearded man. 'If the wound is deep, it can numb the brain and paralyse the memory.'

'My head has not been wounded, yet I feel as though my brain has been numbed for some time,' said the man with the bag.

The bearded man tried to explain, 'It happens in such circumstances; one gets petrified ...' He stopped, startled, mid-sentence, and for a while sat motionless as though he was straining to hear something. Then he looked questioningly towards the man with the bag and asked, 'Isn't it the same sound?'

The man with the bag pricked his ears and said, 'Yes, it is.'

The three strained to catch the sound, looked fearfully at each other and continued to gaze in mute terror. The man with the beard got to his feet. The man with the bag and the youth also stood up. As they began to walk away, the man with the wounded head opened his eyes. Grimacing in pain, he too got to his feet and began to walk behind them. They walked far – first in one direction, then the other. Then they were surprised. The man with the bag said, 'There is no one here for miles around.'

The bearded man said, 'But surely there is someone here because the dog barks again and again.'

'But where is the dog?' asked the youth.

The question caught them unawares. No one had thought of this. Why had none of them yet seen a dog?

The man with the bag said, 'Now the dog too has become a mystery.'

The bearded man said, 'It isn't the dog that's a mystery; it's the man.'

The man with the wounded head interjected in a tone of utter disinterest, 'As long as you can tell the difference between the two.'

The bearded man ignored his sally and turned around. 'Let us go back.'

'Why?'

'It is not wise to go any further.'

And so they turned back. They continued to walk in silence, and reached the spot from which they had started out. The youth sat down and spoke in a tone laced with terror, 'Are we following him, or is he following us?'

'What makes you think that he is following us?' asked the man with the bag, fear in his voice.

'I say that because, when we were turning back, I had felt as though someone were coming behind us every step of the way.'

'Did you turn to look?'

'No.'

The old man with the beard lauded the youth, 'That was sensible of you, young man! One should never look back.'

The man with the wounded head, who had slumped against the tree as soon as they had returned, now got up with a start. He opened his eyes wide and stared at the youth. He said, 'It happened to me too. When I set out to look for him, I had felt as though someone was following me with rapid, long strides when I turned back.'

The bearded man said in a worried tone, 'But my friend, you should have said that at the time.'

'I had forgotten it, but now that this young man has said it, I remember it.' He stopped suddenly as though struck by something.

'What happened? What is wrong?'

'Wait, let me think.' He tried in vain to remember something. Giving up, he said, 'Friends, think carefully and tell me … when I was counting, did I count myself?'

'Count yourself?' the man with the bag asked in a daze.

The man with the wounded head thought for a moment, then said, 'Maybe I didn't count myself … Yes, I am sure I didn't. I forgot to count myself.'

The other three were a bit flummoxed. They said, 'So?'

'So, the man who is missing is me.'

'You?' They were shocked.

'Yes, me.'

They looked at the man with the wounded head in stunned silence. The youth was the first to come to with a start. He suddenly remembered that he too had not counted himself when he was counting the others. He said, 'The man who is missing is me.'

Hearing this, the man with the bag too remembered that while counting the others, he had failed to count himself. He figured he must be the missing man.

The bearded man was lost in thought. After much deliberation, he said, 'I counted all the others while I was counting, but forgot myself. So, obviously, I must be the missing man.'

By now everyone was confounded. The question was: Who was the missing person? The man with the wounded head was once again reminded of the time when he had gone looking for the missing person and had had to return alone. 'At that time, I felt that he was somewhere close beside me, but I wasn't here.'

The bearded man spoke as though he was trying to explain something very elementary, 'But you are here, my friend.' Upon hearing these words, the man with the wounded head looked at each of his companions as though he could not bring himself to trust the bearded man's words. Each of the men convinced him that he was, he was truly there. Finally, he drew a long, shuddering breath and said, 'Because you bear witness to my presence here, I must be here. How sad it is that I must rely on the testimony of others for my being.'

The bearded man said, 'Friend, be thankful that there are three men to bear witness for you. Think of those who once existed but whom no one bore witness for. Now they have ceased to exist.'

The man with the wounded head said, 'You mean if you go back on your testimony, I will cease to exist?'

These words had a profound effect on the others. Each man had the lurking fear in his heart: Am I the missing person? And each man agonized: If I am the missing man, do I exist or not? Their eyes betrayed the fear in their hearts. They looked at each other, then haltingly, fearfully, voiced their doubts. Each bolstered the others' spirits. Each bore witness to the others' presence. Bearing witness to the others' presence and hearing their testimony, they were content. But the youth once again fell into doubt. 'This is very odd … just because we stand witness to each other means that we are … that we exist.'

The man with the wounded head laughed. The others asked, 'Friend, why do you laugh?' The man with the wounded head said, 'I laughed because it occurred to me that I can bear witness to others, but I cannot be my own witness.'

These words once again left them bewildered. A strange doubt held them enthralled. They began to count themselves all over again. This time they began by first counting themselves in. At the end of each exercise, they were still befuddled and asked the others, 'Did I count myself?'

First, one tripped the other's calculations, then, the other tripped a third, and the third tripped the fourth person's calculations. Finally, the youth asked, 'After all, how many of us were there?' The question pierced their hearts. Each one asked the other, after all, how many of us were here? The bearded man heard them out and said, 'Dear friends, all I know is that when we started out, we were all accounted for and no one was missing. Gradually our numbers dwindled until we could be counted on our fingers.

'Things came to such a pass that we lost faith in our own fingers. We counted our numbers again and again, but always came up one short. Then each of us remembered our mistake and started counting all over again to find that we ourselves were missing.'

The youth spoke in a disbelieving tone, 'Have we all gone missing, then?'

The bearded man glared at the youth, angry at him for once again tangling the skein that had just been disentangled. 'No one is missing; we are all accounted for.'

The youth once again asked in a coarse, uncouth manner, 'But how can we tell that we are all accounted for? After all, how many of us were there to begin with?'

'*When* do you mean?' the bearded man asked furiously.

'When we set out.'

The man with the wounded head stared at the youth. 'When did we set out?'

The youth stared back at the man with the wounded head. His eyes welled up. He said, 'I cannot remember when we set out. All I can remember is that the house was filled with smoke and my father was sitting on his prayer rug. His eyes were closed, his lips were moving and his fingers were on the beads.'

The man with the wounded head was still staring, transfixed, at the youth. Then he spoke yearningly, 'Young man, you remember a lot. I don't remember a thing any more.'

The youth spoke sorrowfully, 'But I cannot remember where she was at that instant.'

The bearded man grew tearful and said, 'If only we could remember where we had set out from, when and under what circumstances!'

'And why,' the youth added.

'Yes, and why we had set out,' the bearded man stressed, as though this was something he had momentarily forgotten and the youth had reminded him of it.

The youth scoured his memory and said, 'If I had really set out from Jehanabad, all I remember now is that the rainy season had passed and the koel had left the mango orchards and the swing had been taken off the neem tree in our courtyard.' He became lost in his own thoughts. His voice lowered until it sounded as though he were talking to himself, 'But she continued to come to our house even after the swing had been taken down.' And his thoughts took him further and further away, back to the rain-drenched days when the yellow neem fruit carpeted the ground and when, perched on her swing, she would soar higher and higher and sing: Little drops of rain/My swing sways in the rain. 'But she had continued to come to our house even after the rains … Yes, yes … absolutely … but where was she that day?' He tried his hardest to remember. Then he grew weary and said, 'I cannot remember where she was that day.'

The man with the wounded head kept staring at the youth.

The man with the bag asked, 'What if you didn't leave Jehanabad?'

'What do you mean?' The youth stared in open-mouthed surprise.

'For instance, as our respected elder said, what if we had set out from Gharnata?' the man with the bag spoke in a tone that implied that this was a ridiculously funny idea and that he was actually poking fun at the bearded man. Still, the youth took it seriously and pondering it, said, 'From Gharnata?' He thought some more and said somewhat sadly, 'If I had indeed set out from Gharnata, I do not remember a thing.'

'If we did indeed set out from Gharnata,' the bearded man started speaking in a subdued tone, fell silent, then spoke haltingly again, 'I remember it was the flush of early morning and the minaret of Masjid-e-Aqsa ...'

A crack of laughter escaped the man with the bag. 'The minaret of Masjid-e-Aqsa in Gharnata!'

Flustered, the bearded man lapsed into a nervous silence. The youth looked uncomprehendingly at the bearded man. 'Masjid-e-Aqsa?' he mumbled. Then he too fell silent.

The man with the wounded head could take no more. He said, 'I am heartily sick of this. How does it help me to remember the conditions under which we left, or in which season, or even the name of the city we left behind?'

'Yes, what difference does it make to remember those conditions or the name of that mosque.' The bearded man sighed. 'Still, it would have been nice if we could remember when we had left or where we had left from.'

'And why we left,' the youth interjected.

'Yes, and that too.'

'And also,' the youth went on, 'how many of us there were when we set out.'

The bearded man spoke in an explanatory tone, 'Our numbers were just right then.'

The youth absorbed these words, then asked, 'Was he with us when we set out?'

'Who?' asked the bearded man.

'He who is now no longer with us.'

'Who?' The bearded man looked astonished. 'There was no such person.'

No such person? One looked at the other, the other looked at the third. There was astonishment and there was fear among them. They sat in bewildered silence.

They sat as though they would never speak again.

Finally, the youth stirred. He pricked his ears, trying to catch a sound. The others saw him straining to hear something; they too strained their ears. They sat attentively, trying to catch the faintest sound.

'Is someone there?' the youth whispered.

'Yes, my friends, there is someone close by and that is why the dog is barking,' the man with the bag said.

The four men looked at each other. Then the youth spoke softly, 'What if it is him?'

'Who?'

'Him.'

The bearded man glared at the youth, then stopped to think. Suddenly, something occurred to him and he got to his feet with a start. The others also stood up. They began to walk in the direction from which the sound had come.

The Wall[1]

'He is laughing.'

'What?' Suddenly, everyone turned to look at Gibran's face.

Once again, Gibran strained his ears to try and hear something, then said, 'Yes, yaar. This sounds like laughter. He is laughing.'

Everyone strained their ears to catch that distant sound and – with their worried looks and anxious silence – lent their approval to Gibran's testimony. There was only one person who was not a part of this gloom. His silence was coloured by disinterest rather than dismay. Mandaris, who was the eldest among them, tried his best to not let his anxiety overcome his stature. With immense dignity, he muttered in a sorrowful tone, 'He too ...' and fell silent.

Suddenly, a shudder ran through Ameer's body and he got to his feet. His friends remained sitting and looked at him with questioning eyes.

[1] Published as 'Deevar', in *Kachhuwe*, Sang-e-Meel Publications, Lahore, 2011.

'I will go and get some news,' he said and went away.

The others kept sitting silently. Dusk was falling. Their eyes followed Ameer, yet they could not keep him in sight very long, but the gathering darkness could not stop the sound from travelling. Their ears were tuned to the distant sound.

'Now there is no sound at all,' said Asahil.

Gibran cocked his ears and tried to listen intently. Agreeing with Asahil, he said, 'Yes! Now there is no sound. It seems as though he has stopped laughing.'

Then they heard footsteps. They saw Ameer coming back. No one said anything. No one asked anything. The question lay not on their lips but in their eyes. Their questioning eyes surrounded Ameer.

'But he is not there.'

'What?' And once again they were startled.

'Yes! My friends, he is not there. I went close to that long boundary and looked from one end to the other. He was not there.'

'So he too ...' Mandaris spoke in his majestic but sombre tone, and fell silent.

'But where did he go?' asked Asahil, sounding worried.

'Where those who had gone before him would have gone,' Mandaris answered gravely. And his solemnity seemed to have sealed the lips of his friends. All of them stayed silent. After a long time, Asahil muttered, 'So many of our friends went this way and got lost. The strange thing is that every friend announces that he will go there and come back with some news, but the moment he scales the wall, it is as if a lock is placed on his tongue. And then instead of looking towards us, he looks in the other direction, laughs loudly and goes over to the other side.'

'What is on the other side?' Asahil asked.

'The other side?' Startled, everyone looked at each other with questioning eyes and fell into deep thought – everyone except Amasa.

Mandaris saw Amasa look unperturbed and asked, 'O Amasa, do you know what lies on the other side?'

'There is nothing worth knowing on the other side.'

'Nothing? Then what does everyone go to look at, and why does he laugh?' Ameer asked angrily.

'He laughs when he sees there is nothing there to see.'

This enraged Ameer even more. He got to his feet and said, 'I shall scale the wall and come back and tell you what lies on the other side.'

Worried, his friends looked at him and saw that he was on his feet and ready to go towards the wall.

'Those who left before you said the same thing,' Amasa said with a laugh laced with poison.

'But I shall come back,' Ameer said angrily and set off swiftly. Soon, he disappeared from sight as he had set off with rapid strides and the darkness too was falling fast. His friends watched him go till as far as the eye could see; then, straining their ears, they sat down in fearful silence and waited to hear the same sound that they had heard several times before.

Gibran tried to listen intently and then said, 'There, he too …'

'What? He too?' The friends were startled.

Once again, Gibran tried to listen carefully to that distant sound and said, 'Yes, he too!'

Each of the friends tried, in his own intent way, to listen to the sound and then spoke in fearful tones, 'He too.'

And then the sound ceased. Gibran tried to cock his ears as best as he could, but he could not hear anything. Disappointed, he said, 'Now there is no sound at all.'

'That means he has gone,' Mandaris said.

'What else can it mean?'

Everyone sat quietly for a long time. Finally, Asahil twitched and jerked his body and spoke, 'If only we had the tongue of Yajooj and Majooj.'[2]

---

[2] Yajooj and Majooj are tribes who find a mention in the Quran; being quarrelsome and rapacious they were imprisoned behind a high wall by Zul Qarnain, the just ruler. They could not scale the high wall except on the appointed day by Allah's will. In a Hadith, according to Bukhari, '...every day Yajooj and Majooj break (dig) through the wall erected by Zul Qarnain (A.S.) until they reach the end of it to the extent that they can actually see the light on the other side. They then return (home) saying that "We will break through tomorrow." But Allah causes the wall to revert to its original thickness and the next day they start digging through the wall all over again, and this process continues each day as long as Allah wills them to remain imprisoned. When Allah wishes them to be released, then at the end of the day they will say, "If Allah wills, tomorrow we will break through." The following day they will find the wall as they had left it the previous day (i.e., it will not have returned to its original state) and after breaking the remaining part of it they will emerge.' Yajooj and Majooj (also known as Gog and Magog in the Biblical

'How would that help?' Amasa asked in amazement.

'Then we would have licked the wall down at night.'

'But then it would come back in place the next morning,' Amasa answered dejectedly.

'We would lick it down again.'

'And the next morning it would rise again.'

Mandaris tried to intervene by speaking in his elderly manner, 'Dear ones, do not fight amongst yourselves! Put your heads together and try to find a solution to this business of the wall.'

'It would be better if we were to go back,' Gibran said.

Asahil looked hard at Gibran and said, 'What did you say? Go back?'

'Yes, go back. Our safety lies in going back, or else this wall will bring terrible misfortunes upon us.'

'Going back will bring terrible things upon us.'

'Those terrible things will be much better than this,

---

tradition) were agriculturalists and had presumably tried to break the wall with tools or implements. Interestingly, this incident, which finds a mention in the Quran, has over the centuries become a parable for troublesome people who are destined to pull a wall down all night long for the rest of their lives with little else than their tongues. All night they lick away at the wall till only a paper-thin barrier remains and leave it for the next day. The next morning their night's work is gone and the wall is back in place; the following night they must start the process of licking the wall all over again; this they must do till the Day of Judgement. Intizar Husain has devoted an entire story to this duo and the futility of their eternal task; the story called 'Raat' is included in the collection, *Kachhuwe*.

where one by one we will climb the wall with a prayer and a declaration on our lips, then laugh a meaningless laugh and, without uttering another word, jump off the wall to the other side. After all, what purpose can such an act serve?'

Mandaris drew a long breath and said, 'Dear ones, I can see that this wall has erected walls between us. Before these walls rise any higher, we should find a solution to this problem. Therefore, my dear ones, I have decided that I shall climb the wall myself.'

'Mandaris! You?' everyone asked in alarm.

'Yes, I … I shall climb the wall and bring you news of the other side.'

'It is the same declaration,' said Gibran, 'which the others who have gone so far had made. They made the same declaration, but never returned.'

'But I have thought of a way to return.'

'And what is that?'

'I shall take a long rope and tie one end of it around my waist and put the other end in your hands, and then I shall climb the wall. When I fall victim to the laughter and am about to jump to the other side, all of you must pull at the rope; that way I shall not be able to jump across, and will return with news of what lies on that side.' Amasa heard this and laughed instinctively, but Mandaris turned his eyes away from him and put his plans into action. He wrapped one end of a long rope around his waist and tightly tied a knot, and gave the other end to his friends and set off in the direction of the wall.

Before climbing the wall, Mandaris looked at Gibran

and Asahil who were gripping the rope tightly. He looked at Amasa who was standing some distance away and said, 'O Amasa, will you still stand aloof and let me fall to the other side of the wall?'

Amasa paused for a moment and then moved forward lethargically; he gripped the rope and said, 'I feel sorry for myself for I know exactly how futile and meaningless this endeavour is, and yet I am a party to it.'

Mandaris climbed the wall swiftly. Within the blink of an eye, Gibran and Asahil saw Mandaris standing on top of the wall and looking over the other side. Asahil called out, 'O Mandaris, tell us, what do you see on the other side of the wall?'

Asahil's voice echoed in the gathering darkness and got lost in the wilderness. Asahil was surprised that he had called Mandaris and Mandaris had not responded. Then Gibran called Mandaris, and was surprised that Mandaris did not answer his call either.

'It is most odd that Mandaris can hear our calls and yet he is silent.'

'Mandaris will not answer, for he has seen what lies beyond,' Amasa muttered.

'But,' Gibran said, startled, 'he is laughing.'

'What?' Asahil pricked up his ears. 'Is Mandaris laughing?'

Both listened intently and were surprised and fearful. Mandaris – in whom they had put their faith – had also begun to laugh.

'Mandaris too?' Gibran asked with anxiety.

'No. Mandaris must come back at all costs for he is tied

to the rope and we are holding one end of it tightly in our hands.'

'But, Asahil, my fists are becoming heavy.'

'O Gibran, hold tightly to the rope, for that is the only way we can stop Mandaris from jumping over to the other side.'

Asahil and Gibran, along with Amasa, held tightly to the rope. At first, Mandaris laughed softly, then the sound of his laughter increased till it turned into a long guffaw. Fearfully, Asahil, Gibran and Amasa listened to that long peal of laughter till their fists seemed to grow even heavier.

'Friends, pull the rope towards you, or else we will get pulled towards the wall,' Asahil said.

With all their might, they pulled at the rope until they felt as though they had pulled Mandaris back on their side. But when they went close, their eyes flew wide open with surprise and fear.

Gibran spoke up, 'Friends, what is this that we are seeing ... half of Mandaris's bloodied torso is lying here. Where is the other half of his body?'

'I think that in all that pulling and tugging, half the body came to our side and the other half fell on the other side.'

Gibran heard Asahil's words but hesitated; then he turned towards Amasa and said, 'O Amasa, what do you have to say about this?'

Amasa laughed. 'Mandaris has turned himself into an object of ridicule over a pointless exercise ... look at him ... half his body is lying here and half on the other side.'

Asahil looked at the torn body of Manadaris, soaked

in blood and gore, and spoke in pain.'If only we had the tongues of Yajooj and Majooj.'

'What would have happened then?' Asahil asked, as though stung.

'Then we could have licked this wall down at night.'

'And the next morning it would have come up again.'

'We would lick it down again at the night.'

'And the next morning again it would be back in place,' Amasa said in a sour tone and laughed his poison-laced laughter, and kept on laughing.

Gibran and Asahil were shocked.

'Amasa too …' And Gibran could say no more.

'And he has not even climbed the wall,' Asahil spoke wonderingly.

Asahil and Gibran looked at Amasa with fear and wonderment, as his laughter rose and rose till it turned into a long guffaw.

Reserved Seat[1]

✿

'I don't know what to make of this! Whenever I have a dream, I see dead people – nothing but dead people! God knows which graves they crawl out of! Take my latest one; at first, I could barely sleep. I tossed and turned till late into the night. Sleep just wouldn't come! I must have drifted off at the time of the fajir prayer. And what do I see ... Ahmadi Bua! I had all but forgotten her. People are dead and gone and sleeping under mounds of earth ... how many can one remember? So there I was, perplexed, wondering where Ahmadi Bua cropped up from, and looking so young too! How handsome she looked sitting there, holding the betel-nut chopper in her hand, and the paandan open in front of her. *Katr-katr-katr ...* she chopped the betel nut into tiny pieces. I started asking her ... Ai Ahmadi Bua ... I had barely opened my mouth when another lady showed up. I couldn't recognize her. Suddenly, there was a swarm of ladies – dressed from head to toe in white – when abruptly my eyes opened and I woke up.'

---

[1] Published as 'Reserved Seat' in the collection *Sheherzad ke Naam*, Sang-e-Meel Publications, Lahore, 2002.

Badi Boo fell silent. Then she mumbled softly, 'God alone knows why I only ever see dead people in my dreams. Not that they ever do me any harm. What can they take from me? If anything, they always give me something. Last Thursday, what do I see … Mamman Phupha has come. He's giving me something. And I am saying: Mamman Phupha, what will I do with so much? He is saying: Take it; the children will eat. And, suddenly, I wake up.'

This was no solitary occurrence. Badi Boo invariably narrated some dream or the other every day. It never ceased to surprise us that she could have so many dreams and always saw only dead people in them. She herself was surprised by the easy familiarity the dead seemed to have with her. So many ancestors, close and distant, would come to her in her dreams and they always gave her something. We came to know everything about our dead ancestors through her dreams – how they were related to us, when they had died and where they were buried. There were some who had crossed the seas and died in strange lands. God knows what magic spell Badi Boo brewed that the dead from distant lands invariably showed up in her dreams. 'And what do I see … my aunt-in-law's husband has come. He's the one who had gone away and joined the firangi's army in Rangoon. I had always seen my aunt-in-law living all alone, though the money orders came regularly every month. Then we heard he died there. So, naturally, I was puzzled … how did he come here all the way from Rangoon? And he's saying to me: "So, bahu, are you well? See, what I've got for you from Rangoon" … and just as he is about to take something out of a bundle, my eyes open and I am awake.'

It was invariably like this. She would wake up at the very moment when someone was about to give her something. Even so, the dead had given her so much in her dreams that, in her waking moments, had the living given her even a fraction of all that she got from them, she would have been blessed with immense riches. But she considered herself sufficiently blessed that all the dead who came to her in her dreams always wanted to give her something. She looked so pleased after every dream.

Once, she had a dream that left her a little perturbed: 'Arre, last night I had such a peculiar dream that I woke up with goose bumps! There is a house ... not this one ... some other ... I don't know whose. It is a very strange house with a room large enough to hold a village common. In the middle of the room, someone is lying on a bed, sleeping perhaps, covered from head to toe with a sheet. I am saying to myself: Ya Allah, who can it be, asleep like this? I go to the next room and see Nanhi Bua coming towards me. She's saying: "Come, Asghari, come with me. I have come to take you." So saying, she clutches my hand and starts walking rapidly. I nearly die of fright, but I manage to loosen her grip on my hand and cry: "Leave my hand. I don't want to go with you." I'm scared. I free my hand and run. There is utter darkness ahead of me. And then, I wake up.'

For a while, Badi Boo looked lost in thought, then she said in a worried tone: 'Allah alone knows the meaning hidden in this dream. I simply entrusted it to the care of

Imam Zaman.[2] I always do that, you know, hand all my worrying dreams to the care of Imam Zaman.' She paused, then spoke as though she had been thinking a lot about it. 'Now there is no one left to transcribe my dreams. Bade Abba, may Allah grant him Paradise, was so good at transcribing dreams that whatever he told you always came true. Look at me, remembering dreams from so long ago! Once, I had dreamt that someone had dropped a banana in my lap, a long banana with a green skin. And I was wondering who could have dropped it in my lap. The next day I narrated the dream to Bade Abba. He told me not to talk about it to anyone else. God willing, you are going to give birth to a son, he said. It was the month of Ramzan and I was expecting a baby. It was my eighth month. The next month Murtaza was born.'

Badi Boo had an incredible memory. She remembered all her dreams, old and new. When she didn't have a new dream to tell, she would open her casket of old dreams and tell us several dreams at one go. But these were invariably other people's dreams. Sometimes it would be Bade Abba's dream, or else Phuphi Amma's or Majhli Khala's. 'Arre, the Hindu-Muslim riots broke out much later. Bade Abba had seen it all in his dreams before it started – at a time when no one could have imagined that there would be such devastation and havoc. How worried Bade Abba had been the day he had his dream! He had said to me: "What a strange dream! There is

---

[2] Imam Zaman is believed by Shia Muslims to be the twelfth and final imam who will be the ultimate saviour of humankind.

a long thorn lying right across our inner courtyard," and I asked in a worried tone, "Who could have flung it here?" He was quiet for a minute, then he said, "It is an inauspicious dream. May God have mercy on all of us!"'

And so she carried on – sometimes narrating her own dreams, sometimes retelling the dreams of our long-dead ancestors. Every day, it would be a new dream. Once, she had the most incredible dream. 'It is as though there is a railway station. Coolies are rushing about, shouting. Trains are steaming in and out. There is much scurrying about among the passengers. Someone is balancing a bedroll on his head, someone else is getting a coolie to carry his trunks when, suddenly, the train chugs in. The passengers rush to get in. In all that pushing and pulling and shoving and jostling, I somehow manage to get into a compartment. And what do I see ... Saiyadani Bi is sitting right there, at a window seat. I am amazed to see her there because she has been dead for so long that her bones must have turned to dust in her grave. What is she doing here? And sitting close beside her is that slut to beat all sluts – Billo! And look at her – staring at me with those saucer-like eyes of hers! What a brazen hussy! The number of homes she broke and the fights she caused between so many husbands and wives! Had she lived some more, God alone knows how many divorces she would have caused. Saiyadani Bi makes a gesture towards me and I am about sit down on an empty seat near her when suddenly the Ticket Babu materializes out of thin air, demanding to see my ticket. I say: Here it is. He looks at my ticket and says: Amma, there is no seat reserved for you here. I say: Son, make me a reservation if there isn't one. There is an empty seat over here; I will take that. He says: But this seat is reserved for someone else. I say: Do you expect me to stand all the way? He says: Amma-ji, there are no more vacant seats on this train. You will have to get off. I grumble: Ai, hai, what will I do if I get off? He answers: There is another train coming soon after this one; it has lots of place. You will find a seat. How I plead and weep and moan, but that wretched man will hear none of it. He makes me get off the train. The train chugs out of the station in front of my eyes. It is bursting at the seams. Every face that I can see belongs to a dead person I had once known. I am amazed. Suddenly there is a loud whistle – it pierces my eardrums and the train ... the train has disappeared!'

Badi Boo fell silent. Then she mumbled, half to herself: 'God alone knows the meaning hidden behind this dream.' Then, after a long introspection, she said, as though she had stumbled upon its meaning: 'I think there is a sign here, a sign from the Other World, saying: Asghari, your time has come. You must stay ready now. But what readiness do I need? I have been sitting here, ready for so long.'

From then on, it was as though the dream had caught Badi Boo in its spell. She would find excuses to dwell upon it time and again. 'I know that my time has come. Any day now, the summons will come. The signal has already been given; it is only a matter of the summons reaching me. How I long for the day when they will finally reach me! I am ready and waiting for it.'

'No, no, Badi Boo, you are not going anywhere. You have a long life ahead of you.'

'Ai, hai, haven't I lived enough! Do you want me to be around to lug the sacks of misdeeds on the Day of Judgement?' And once again, she would plunge into inconsolable grief. 'Abba Miyan went away. Then Amma passed away. Bade Bhaiya, too, went to sleep under mounds of earth. Everyone has gone. I am the only shameless one left behind to mourn them. No, no, I won't wait any more. May the Caller call me as soon as He pleases!'

Badi Boo lived in desperate wait for her next dream. She was convinced that, any day now, she would have another dream in which the second train that the rail babu had spoken of would come – *chuk-chuk-chuk*. She would mumble: 'Why is it taking so long? I am sitting here, all packed and ready to go. I will go the minute the train shows up.' But strangely enough, where once she invariably had some dream or the other every night, now she had simply stopped dreaming. She grew steadily more anxious.

Sometimes she would begin to blame herself: 'It is my fault; I should have held my ground and wedged myself right next to Saiyadani Bi. What could the ticket babu have done? He could hardly have lifted me bodily and thrown me out on the platform! And look at that Saiyadani Bi – she was loath to make the slightest protest on my behalf! She didn't say a word, simply looked on with those big eyes of hers. Had she held my hand and made me sit down, perhaps it would have bolstered my courage, and I would have given that rail babu such a tongue-lashing that he would have remembered it all his life. But who can one blame? I am the one at fault. I let the moment slip.'

'It was a good thing you did, Badi Boo. You are the only elder we have; what would we do with you gone?'

'May you live a thousand years, my precious ones! May you know every happiness! But the old must go; how long can they tarry? I am only waiting for the train; I will leave as soon as it comes.'

The train had become so much a part of Badi Boo's every waking moment that she talked of nothing else. Soon, she fell ill. She had been ill before, but this time it seemed as though she had chosen to fall sick with the express intention of dying. She declared that, this time, she would not remain alive for very long, so we might as well not bother with doctors or medicines. Call Murtaza; that was her only plea. 'How can I go without seeing his face one last time? After all, he is the one who has to lower me into the grave.'

We had known for some time now that Badi Boo had implacably resolved to die. By now most of us believed that her end was near and we really ought to inform Murtaza Mamu. A letter was duly dispatched, conveying in Badi Boo's inimitable style the hopelessness of the situation and the urgent need for Murtaza Mamu to show up at his dying mother's bedside. 'Come quickly, my dearest one, before my eyes close forever. My dying wish is to see my precious son's face one last time before I leave this earth. My eyes are glued to the door. My spirit may leave this body, but my eyes won't close till you come.'

After this, Badi Boo's gaze never left the door. The train that she had once awaited so anxiously now faded into the background. She began a restless vigil for her son. One anxious wait had replaced another. 'God knows when he will come! How I had dreaded this moment! How I had pleaded with him not to go across the seven seas! How will you come when your mother is on her deathbed, I had said. Get yourself transferred here. There is no knowing when I will die. I can be called at any moment. How will you reach in time?'

Anyhow, Murtaza Mamu reached well in time, even though by Badi Boo's reckoning he was far too late in coming. If anything, Murtaza Mamu was actually too early. The sight of her son and grandson gave Badi Boo a fresh lease of life. She sat up as though she had never been ill for a moment!

Murtaza Mamu had brought his son, Artaza, with him. Masha Allah, how big he had grown! He had been a slip of a lad, kicking the dust in the alleys, when he had lived here. He used to be inseparable from his catapult. Badi Boo used to admonish him for taking potshots at the poor, harmless little birds. 'May the Lord save you from the moment of ill omen! Birds, too, are of all kinds; some can even bring you ill luck. It's not good to harm them.' But Artaza never paid heed. His ears and eyes were slaves to his catapult. But now he had grown up, and, Masha Allah, grown up to be a tall, strapping young man. He had also sobered down considerably. Now all his energies were focused on his studies. He had completed his BA and started his MA. Badi Boo looked at him, cracked her knuckles over her own head to take upon herself all his misfortunes and said to her son, 'Murtaza, may Satan turn a deaf ear to what I am about to say, but it is time now to get Artaza married. Look for a suitable girl for him.'

'Married?' Murtaza Mamu asked, as though without a care in the world. 'Let him finish his studies.'

'His studies have become endless like the devil's intestines! What will happen if all the nice girls slip out of our hands by the time he finishes his studies?'

'What can we do? Allah is the One who does everything.'

'Of course He does, but we too must think about it. And, son, think of me. My one last wish is to see the sehra tied around my grandson's forehead before I close my eyes forever.'

We were delighted to hear this because Badi Boo, without any prompting from anyone, had decided to make an appropriate extension to her life span.

Badi Boo didn't care what a BA or MA meant; she was proud that the father had given sufficient importance to the son's religious education. It pleased her no end to see that Artaza was well versed in matters of religious law and practice and was punctual with his namaaz. Perhaps he had become more punctilious since coming here. He would unfailingly go to the mosque to offer the fajir prayer. That morning too, he had woken up before the muezzin's call – unlike his other friends who were still asleep – and set off for the mosque. That was the day the father and son were supposed to return home. Murtaza Mamu's leave was coming to an end and Badi Boo too, by the Grace of God, was getting better. In fact, she had stopped all her medicines saying, 'These wretched, gall-bitter, modern-day medicines refuse to go down my throat any more. I am all right now. Enough of these modern whimsies! How long do you people intend to rock me in a cradle like a newborn baby?' And so she had risen from her sickbed and started moving about. Soon enough, she was chattering away like she used to. For so many days now, she hadn't even had a dream. She barely had time to remember her old dreams. The dead had visited her in the guise of her dreams. So, now, they too had vanished. You can say the dead had departed from the world of her imagination. A new life tempted her. The sehra on her grandson's forehead swam delightfully before her eyes. She had already started looking for a suitable bride. She ran through a list of almost all the marriageable girls, both from within the family and outside. She analysed the looks and character of each one in minute detail. She would say that she would get such a lovely bride for her Artaza that no one could match her – not even if they set out with a magical lamp to look for another such damsel!

Soon, the day of departure dawned. That day Artaza had woken up before the muezzin's call and rushed towards the mosque. Badi Boo, too, had woken up at the crack of dawn. She had once again started saying her fajir prayers at the prescribed time.

Badi Boo was still seated on her prayer mat when she heard a commotion in the neighbourhood; she mumbled, 'May the good Lord keep us safe from misfortune, what is this noise?'

But the misfortune had already struck. The congregation had barely gathered in the mosque when a couple of Kalashnikov-toting masked men barged in and sprayed the devout with bullets. Some of those who had bowed their heads in supplication never raised their head again.

People heard the gunshots and raced towards the mosque. Some neighbours brought Artaza home. He was drenched in blood. A doctor was sent for, but Artaza's time had come. He died before the doctor could reach him.

Badi Boo beat her chest inconsolably. She cursed herself for asking her son to bring Artaza along. Then she cursed the terrorists. May they die a terrible death! The monsters had no reverence even for the House of God! The scoundrels, what sort of Musalmans were they that they couldn't even let the boy complete his namaaz? And she burst into loud sobs and began to cry like a baby.

In the middle of her tears, she suddenly remembered her dream about the train and sat stock-still. 'Oh my God! At that time, I couldn't understand what the rail babu was trying to say. He was saying, Maa-ji, this seat is not meant for you; it is reserved for someone else. And at that very moment someone came and sat down in the reserved seat. It was a boy. But I was so engrossed in my own troubles that I didn't pay any heed. How was I to know who it was! I should have seen who it was who had sat down in my place. '

Badi Boo once again started beating her chest and howling with grief. 'Hai, I was left behind; he went away.'

Clouds[1]

He wandered far in search of the clouds. He walked down several winding paths and alleys until he reached the old mud hut. From there he took the dirt track that skirted the fields. A grass-cutter was coming from the other direction, carrying a bundle of freshly cut grass on his head. He stopped him and asked, 'Did you see the clouds there?'

'Clouds?' The grass-cutter was amazed, as though he had been asked the most unexpected question.

'Yes, clouds.' But when there was no lessening of the grass-cutter's surprise, he felt disappointed. He walked on until he reached a farmer ploughing his field. He asked the farmer the same question: 'Did the clouds come here?'

The farmer too couldn't make head or tail of this. Taken aback, he spluttered, 'Clouds?'

'Yes, clouds.'

He was asking about the clouds like one who has lost a child and asks wayfarers if they have seen it wandering

---

[1] First published as 'Baadal' in the short story collection *Kachhuwe*, Sang-e-Meel Publications, Lahore, 1995.

about. Perhaps the clouds, too, were lost children and he was going around asking people about them, but no one could give him a satisfactory answer.

His mother was the first person he had asked in the morning. 'Amma-ji, where did the clouds go?'

'Who went where?' Amma-ji asked as though he had asked an exceptionally stupid question.

'Clouds.'

'Clouds! Have you lost your mind, boy? Hurry up now. Quickly wash your hands and face, eat your breakfast and go to school.'

Amma-ji's brusque behaviour had a depressing effect on him. He washed his hands and face dejectedly, ate his breakfast, slung his satchel of schoolbooks around his neck and left home. But as he stepped out, the same question rose in his mind: where did the clouds go? He remembered the sight he had seen the previous night: how the clouds had billowed and surged in the night sky. Yet when he had gone to sleep, the sky had been empty of clouds and spangled with stars. There hadn't been a trace of a breeze and the oppressive heat made it difficult to sleep. After a long time, he had managed to fall asleep. Then, after some time, he had woken up. God knows what the time had been. To him it looked like the middle of the night. Up there in the sky, clouds were rumbling and rolling, gathering momentum. Occasionally, there would be flashes of thunder and peals of lightning, and in those brief moments of illumination, the clouds looked very dense and black. It seemed as though it would rain soon. But the rain would spoil his slumber.

With that thought, he closed his eyes. He pretended he was completely oblivious to the thunder. Soon, he fell asleep. When he got up in the morning, he was amazed. The sky … the sky was clear and empty! There was not a trace of rain in the courtyard. At first he was surprised, then sad. He was surprised that the clouds had surged and scudded across the skies without shedding a drop. And it made him sad to think that he had fallen asleep. Had he stayed awake, perhaps the clouds would not have disappeared like that. Perhaps they would have shed at least some of their rain … if only he had not fallen asleep. Had it rained, it would have been the season's first rainfall. But the clouds had come – massed, billowing, rumbling clouds – and gone away while he slept. Not a drop of rain had fallen from them.

The month of the rains was slipping away. He looked up once again to inspect the skies as he walked along. There wasn't a patch of cloud to be seen anywhere. The sun beat down on his head from a clear, molten sky. He left the road that went to his school and began walking towards the fields.

Walking on the narrow boundaries between the fields, he went far away. The heat was fierce. His body began to burn. His throat was parched. After crossing many fields, he spotted a large tree under whose ample shade a Persian wheel was turning gently. He felt as though he had reached an oasis in the middle of a desert. He reached the shelter of the tree, threw down his satchel of books, splashed the cool water churning out of the Persian wheel on his dusty feet. Then he washed his hands and face and drank the water to his heart's content.

He felt refreshed after washing his hands and face and quenching his thirst. He looked around to inspect his surroundings. An old man sat on a crumbling wall near the edge of the Persian wheel, puffing away at a huqqah. He looked at the old man as though he wanted to say something, but quailed at the prospect. Finally, he plucked up the courage to ask, 'Did the clouds come here?'

The old man puffed at his huqqah, looked closely at him and said, 'Son, the clouds won't come here in disguise. When they come in all their massed splendour, the earth and sky will know of their coming.'

'But the clouds had come last night and no one knew.'

'The clouds came last night?' The old man thought for a moment, then called out in a loud voice, 'Allah Din, did the clouds come last night?'

Allah Din was ploughing the field with his bullock. He stopped and said, 'I fell asleep the moment my back rested against my bed. I don't know.'

The old man said, 'It is not enough for the clouds to come. I once lived in an area where it didn't rain for ten years.'

'Ten years?' He was horrified and his mouth fell open.

'Yes, ten years. The clouds would come. They gathered and rumbled with such force once when I was there, but not a drop of rain fell from them.'

'That is strange.'

'No, there is nothing strange about it. It rains on His command. When He commands it, the clouds drop their rain; when He does not give the command, the clouds do not drop their rain.'

The old man's words conjured up images from many past showers. He remembered dense, black clouds that emerged from black nights with great ferocity, looking as though they would unleash torrential rain, but scudding away without shedding so much as a drop. Then there were also those other clouds that had come in the guise of a few meaningless, seedless tufts, yet let loose such a downpour that it made ponds and lakes brim over.

The old man looked at the smouldering sky and muttered, 'The season is slipping past. When will He give the command?'

He too muttered, as though in answer, 'God knows where the clouds went.'

'Son, either it doesn't rain or, when it does, reports of floods start coming in. The sky has become a miser. The earth does not have the strength any more. Either it doesn't rain, or if it does, it causes floods.'

He could barely understand the old man's words, yet he sat there listening to him. Suddenly he remembered how late it had gotten. He picked up his satchel of schoolbooks, slung it around his neck and got to his feet.

He walked for miles in the sun and dust. He went back on the same dirt tracks he had taken to come here. The sun was still fierce and hot. But by the time he reached the mud hut, he sensed a nip in the air and the earth felt damp beneath his feet.

As he neared the village, he saw the roads were wet, trees that had been draped in the usual layers of dust when he had left in the morning now looked freshly bathed and the little gutter that had been dry since the last monsoon was gurgling like a mountain stream. A wave of happiness coursed through his body. He was in a hurry to get home. He wanted to see how fresh and clean the jamun tree in his courtyard looked.

When he reached home, he saw that the rain had changed everything. A lot of leaves had fallen from the jamun tree and were now lying soiled and a little bruised in the wet earth. The tree stood clean and scrubbed, freshly showered, and Amma-ji was saying in a rare moment of contentment, 'That was a good rain! Thank God for it! The heat was killing me.'

Drops were still falling from the leaves of the jamun tree. He stood beneath the tree and let the drops fall on his head and his face. His eyes lifted towards the sky; it looked clear and scrubbed. There wasn't a trace of a cloud there now. It occurred to him that he had walked so far in the dust and the sun in search of the clouds, and in his absence they had come, shed their rain and gone away. The thought made him sad. The rain-soaked air, redolent with the smell of damp earth, suddenly became meaningless to him.

Needlessly[1]

The wife looked at him and asked, 'Why are you laughing?'

'I am not laughing, am I?' He looked alarmed.

'Not laughing? Why, you are grinning from ear to ear!' She tried to probe, 'Are you remembering someone?'

'Whom would I remember?' he mumbled, then fell quiet.

He tried to make his wife go away so that he could laugh to his heart's content, but she refused to budge.

She put away the breakfast dishes in the kitchen and hurried back. Soon it became very clear that he was not likely to have the freedom to laugh in the house.

Where was he to go?

Weary at the prospect of home, he began to rack his mind for other possibilities. He thought of places he could go where he could laugh in peace. He desperately wanted to laugh today and had planned to sit peacefully at home and laugh.

But now that the chances of being able to laugh at home had grown slim, he stood up to leave.

---

[1] Published as 'Besabab' in short story collection *Kachhuwe*, Sang-e-Meel Publications, Lahore, 1995.

'Weren't you supposed to go late to the office today?' asked the wife pointedly.

'Yes, but I have suddenly remembered some urgent chores. I might as well finish them.'

'Very well. Since you are going out, pay the electricity bill too. The last date is day after tomorrow.' She got up to get the bill and the money.

Just as he was about to leave, she remembered another errand. 'We have to send the money order to Khala Amma. Once you have paid the bill, send the money order from the post office nearby.' She dived in again and returned to hand him a hundred-rupee note.

He drew a long breath of relief as he came out of his house. I can laugh now, he thought. A smile quivered on his lips as he revved his scooter. And close on its heels came the thought: what will people say when they see me riding a scooter and laughing? A man sitting on a scooter and laughing is a strange sight, and with that he straightened his smile and sobered up.

He reached the bank counter to pay the electricity bill and saw a long, snaking queue. He too lined up and grew steadily bored. His turn came, he paid the bill and left for the post office. By the time he had collected the money order form, a long queue was forming here too. He found himself at the end of the line. Finally, this chore too was done.

The bank and the post office had left him thoroughly dejected. He longed to find a cool, quiet spot where he could drink a cup of tea and feel refreshed. He spotted a hotel and went in. He took a gulp of cold water and sighed with relief.

As the hot tea slid down his throat, he felt even better. Once again, he remembered his desire to laugh.

He had to laugh, but he was also aware that the customers at nearby tables would think it very odd to see him sitting alone and laughing. They would think he had lost his marbles. He looked around. All the tables were taken. It was lunch time. People were engrossed in eating. There wasn't a trace of a smile on any face. 'I have finally found the time to laugh, but I am on my own. If a man is alone and laughing, the obvious conclusion to be drawn is that he is mad. So it is imperative to have company in order to laugh. What a strange restriction!'

He figured he might as well go to the office. 'I will never find a better place to laugh. There are always enough people to join in when one laughs. Most of the time is spent in idle chatter – sometimes about politics, sometimes cracking jokes. Faruqi has an inexhaustible fund of jokes; he simply needs an excuse to crack one, and then he can go on forever.'

He reached the office and found things to be not quite normal. The hot topic of discussion was that Faruqi's promotion had been stalled and, in his place, Ali Ahmad had been elevated even though he was much junior to Faruqi. Faruqi's mood was decidedly 'off'.

Helplessly, he left the office to return home. By now he was besieged with one overriding question: why, after all, did he want to laugh?

'Why do I want to laugh?'

And the question brought him to another question: 'Need there be a reason to laugh?'

He remembered that in the morning when his wife had asked, 'Why are you laughing?' the question had left him unnerved.

'To ask why are you doing this at every turn in life, on every occasion – how absurd it is! Surely one should do certain things that are reasonless, meaningless. Why must I ask myself why I laugh or even why I need to laugh? I want to laugh, that's it … For no reason, just like that …'

By now he had sufficiently convinced himself with his own arguments and counter-arguments, but how was he to make others see things his way? Others always ask why one is laughing or crying. As he thought of more reasons to bolster his arguments, he took a look around. Everywhere, he saw at least one thing that could make one laugh. Despite so much material for laughter, why do people always ask 'why' when someone is laughing? And why is it necessary to give a reason: *this* is why I am laughing? It seemed surprising to him that despite the abundance of reasons to laugh, one laughed so rarely … hmm … now he was mocking himself …

He reached home and found things very much in his favour. The state of affairs now was just the opposite of what they had been in the morning. The evening meal was late in being put on the stove. The wife had no time to come and sit beside him. He savoured his solitude. Solitude is very much a thing to be savoured – there is no one to check on you, to see what you are doing. It makes a man feel free, liberated.

Aimlessly, he switched on the radio and equally aimlessly, he twiddled its knobs. He found a station airing a radio play.

The play was a comedy. He listened for a while and felt quite happy. Then he moved to another station. This one was playing songs. Happy songs ...

He did some more surfing. Whichever station he chanced upon, he found programmes of happiness. 'How happy everyone seems!' he said to himself.

'Yes, everyone seems happy, don't they?' he muttered and grew sad. For no reason whatsoever!

The Sage and the Butcher[1]

❦

Once there was a rishi named Kaushik.[2] Even though he
was a rishi, he would often get very angry. And it was no
ordinary sort of anger; he would turn such a wrathful gaze

---

[1] Published as 'Rishi aur Qasai' in *Shabkhun*, Allahabad, June-
December 2005.

[2] Kaushik is probably used here as a generic name as Kaushiks
are among the highest of the Brahmins. This story is possibly inspired
by the *Vyadha Gita* (meaning 'Teachings of a Butcher'), part of the
epic Mahabharata, and consists of the teachings imparted by a
vyadha (butcher) to a Brahmin. In the story, an arrogant sannyasi is
humbled by a *vyadha*, and learns about dharma (righteousness). The
Vyadha Gita teaches that 'no duty is ugly, no duty is impure' and it
is only the way in which the work is done that determines its worth.
Dharmavyadha's name is an ironic one for it means, the 'butcher of
dharma'. Intizar Husain has used more Hindi words in this story than
his other writings and shows a keen and accurate knowledge of not
merely Hindu mythology through his readings of the puranas and the
kathas, but also a grasp of Sanskrit words and their 'corrupted' usage
in the rhythms of daily discourse among ordinary people, words such
as *deekh* for *dakshina*.

on the object of his rage that it would immediately be burned
to cinders. Later, he would at times repent his wrath.

Once it so happened that he was sitting beneath a peepal
tree, immersed in meditation. A poor crane, who had flown
a long distance, spotted the tree and alighted upon it. The
moment he had settled upon a branch, he released a few
pellets of shit. As luck would have it, the rishi was meditating
under that very branch. The droppings fell directly on his
head and disturbed his meditation. It enraged him. He
glanced up and spotted the crane. So *this* creature has caused
the rupture in my meditation, he said to himself and shot
such a wrathful gaze at it that the poor crane immediately
went up in flames, and in a matter of seconds, dropped in
front of him like a lump of burnt-out coal. The sight of the
cinders immediately put out his anger and he was overcome
with remorse. 'The poor bird,' he said to himself, 'it was only
bird droppings after all. It was hardly a sin grave enough
to deserve death. I am such a fool … why did I not stop to
think? I have taken the life of the poor crane!'

Kaushik rishi was genuinely sorrowful at the death of the
crane. He was full of remorse, too. He resolved not to get
angry again. But he would forget the resolution whenever
something enraged him. And later, he would feel sorry for
having given in.

And listen to what happened once … One day, he set out
from his ashram in search of dakshina. When he reached
a village, he walked up to a house and knocked at its door.
The woman of the house was scrubbing dishes. She glanced
towards the door and spotted an old man with matted

white hair and a begging bowl in his hand. She understood that it must be some yogi who had come to ask for alms. She called out, 'Maharaj, please sit patiently for some time. Let me finish scrubbing my pots and pans and then I will serve you.'

And so the rishi sat down in the doorway, prepared to wait for the dakshina. There were so many pots and pans that it was taking forever to scrub and clean them! The moment she had finished washing them all, the woman's husband entered the house. Instantly, she left all her chores and became engrossed in serving her husband. She fetched water to wash the dust off his feet. Then she went into the kitchen to serve his food on a platter and brought it before him. It was a hot day, so she stood in front of him and cooled him with a hand-held fan. The husband asked for water and she instantly ran to get him cool water. The husband lingered over his meal. The wife dotingly served him.

It was only when the husband had finished his meal and gone to sleep that the wife remembered the yogi who had come begging and was waiting by the doorway. She gathered the dakshina and rushed to the door. She said, 'Forgive me, maharaj, you had to wait for so long. I was so engrossed in serving my husband that I almost forgot that you have been waiting for me.'

Kaushik rishi was already annoyed at having been made to wait for such a long time. He listened to the woman's words and his anger climbed several notches. Furious, he said, 'It is good to serve one's husband, but it is also your dharma to serve the Brahmin who comes to your door. I have been waiting here for such a long time! I am a Brahmin, not a beggar!'

The woman looked closely at him. She knew this was Kaushik rishi, a man famous for his temper. Clearly he was in a rage and getting angrier by the minute. The woman fell at his feet and implored him, 'Forgive me, rishi-ji. I have been wrong.'

But the rishi's temper could not be cooled so easily. If anything, his anger rose and rose. So, when the woman saw that the rishi was losing control, she let loose a volley of reprimands. 'Control yourself, rishi-ji,' she said, 'there is no need for such anger. I am no crane that will turn into ashes when you look at me with anger. I am the wife of a Brahmin. My greatest dharma is to serve my husband. In any case, you go around with a thatch growing on your head; is it such a calamity if a bird dropped something on it?'

Kaushik rishi had never imagined that anyone would have the temerity to speak to him in this manner. Taken aback, he wondered who on earth this Brahmin woman might be. Most of all, he was surprised that she knew about the crane. And so he said, 'Woman, you have turned out to be a shrew! How do you know about the crane that was burnt to cinders?'

She replied, 'O rishi, nothing remains hidden. You have turned so many innocent birds to ashes with your anger; how can such a thing remain a secret? Knowledge cannot be confined to that of the vedas and puranas alone; after all, one must also have self-knowledge. He cannot be a learned man who knows all that is contained in the books, but has no control over his own self.'

Kaushik rishi stood before her with folded hands and said, 'O Brahmin lady, you win and I lose. Now I shall seek knowledge from you.'

'I am no teacher or giver of knowledge. I don't have the time. What would I know about such matters? If you desire instruction, go to Mithila and seek refuge at the feet of Dharmavyadha. He will tell you what dharma is and what adharma.'

Kaushik rishi took her advice and set off instantly. With the name of Dharmavyadha on his lips, he took the road to Mithila.

Upon reaching Mithila, he began to enquire about the hermitage of Dharmavyadha. But there was no such hermitage and no one could tell him about it. Everyone expressed their ignorance. Finally, an old man said, 'Are you looking for Dharmavyadha?'

'Yes, I am looking for Dharmavyadha.'

'But Dharmavyadha is a butcher. Why would he have an ashram? Ask for directions to his shop; it is at the turning of the next lane.'

Dharmavyadha was a butcher? It caused no end of perplexity to the rishi. He refused to believe that it could be so. The old man said. 'I have told you where Dharmavyadha can be found; the rest is up to you.'

Rishi-ji found himself in a dilemma: what was he to do? Then he decided, after all, to go and see for himself. He walked to the turning of the next lane. He spotted a meat shop and a butcher with a cleaver in his hand. The man was making mince out of the meat. Kaushik rishi was revolted at the sight. He thought, this cannot possibly be the Dharmavyadha that the Brahmin lady had told him about. He was lost in his thoughts when the butcher saw him and came out of the shop. He touched the rishi's feet and said, 'Rishi-ji, I know. The Brahmin lady told you about me and I have been waiting for you. Come, come with me to my house.'

He reached the man's house and felt as though he had come to an abode of peace. The butcher did not seem like a butcher at all; he appeared to be a model of love, devotion and peace. He explained so many intricacies of dharma to the rishi. Yet a thorn was stabbing the rishi's heart: why was such a devout man a butcher? Finally he could control himself no longer and the question sprang to his lips: 'Maharaj, one thing does not cease to surprise me.'

'And what is that?'

'A wise man like you, steeped in the wisdom of the shastras, runs a knife along the throats of animals every day. You slit their throats, you chop their flesh to pieces, then sell those pieces.'

Dharmavyadha laughed and said, 'Rishi-ji, this world and this life – yours and mine – are nothing but a spectacle. Weeds and herbs, fruits and vegetables, birds and animals – all are fodder for someone or the other. Listen, O rishi, in ancient times there was a king, nay not a king but a god! So good, so kind was he! Every day thousands of animals were killed for his kitchens. Two thousand cows alone were butchered. But only some of this meat would be cooked in his own kitchen; the rest was distributed amongst the poor and the needy.'

'Even cows?' Kaushik rishi's eyes were wide open with surprise. 'But that is very sad!'

'O rishi, every living creature gives dakshina to another living creature; herein lies the secret of life.'

Kaushik rishi remained lost in thought for a long time. After intense deliberation, he spoke. 'O Wise One, are you not a Brahmin?'

'I was; now I am not. But I shall become one again.'

'I don't understand.'

'O rishi, I was a Brahmin in my last birth. I was steeped in the vedas and shastras. Then I became friends with the king. Whenever the king went on a hunt, I too would go with him. The king would kill a lot of deer. One day, emulating the king, I too sighted a deer, aimed an arrow at it and shot it. But when it let out a piercing cry, I found that it was not a deer I had shot, but a man. In fact, he was a rishi; he cursed me that in my next birth I would be a butcher. I was much saddened. I said, "But my skin is a Brahmin's." He replied, "So what? You will soon grow a butcher's skin." Again, I asked, "But how will I get back into my own skin?" He answered. "When you impart learning to a rishi you will get back your own skin." And so I left my mortal body and entered into my next birth and became a butcher. But now that I have granted knowledge to a Brahmin, I can go back into my skin. Now you will become a butcher and I shall go back to being a Brahmin.'

Kaushik rishi was much perplexed upon hearing these words and asked, 'But how will I return to my skin?'

'You will return to your own skin when some self-wronged rishi like yourself comes to sit at your feet and you grant him knowledge. Once that happens, you will return to your own skin and that rishi will take the form of a butcher.'

And with these words, Dharmavyadha changed his form. While he was transformed into a Brahmin, Kaushik rishi became a butcher.

Noise[1]

'So, what do you think? What will happen now?'

'Anything can happen after this.'

'Such as?'

'Such as,' and he fell into deep thought. 'Yaar, there is terrible confusion.' And then he fell silent and began to drink his tea.

I too stayed quiet and kept drinking my tea. I could hear the shout from outside. I perked up my ears, tried to hear as intently as I could and then stood up. 'The *Supplement* has come.' I went out, bought the *Supplement*, returned and opened it on the table; both of us began to read it together.

After I had finished reading it, I asked, 'So, what do you think?'

'Yaar, there was only a snippet; there were no new details.'

'Still, what do you think? What will happen now?'

'What will happen now,' and he fell into deep thought. 'That's a tough question, yaar!'

---

[1] Published as 'Shor' in the collection *Kachchuwe*, Sang-e-Meel Publications, Lahore, 2011.

'Still, what do you think?'

Speaking as though he were in great thought, he began, 'I think ...' Then, looking to either side, he stopped and said, 'Yaar, there is so much noise here!'

I too looked at the tables on either side of us. All the adjacent tables were full. Their occupants were less engrossed in drinking tea and more interested in talking. And the table closest to us was also the loudest. It had fewer teacups and more people. And its occupants were speaking in such loud voices that it was impossible to have a leisurely conversation while they were around.

I was a bit surprised and also angry. Such blithe people ... they were sitting around and talking as though nothing had happened.

I ran my eyes all around the room. I could see a secluded spot near the kitchen with several empty tables.

'Come, let us go and sit there.'

And we got up and sat down in the alcove near the kitchen. It was indeed a very peaceful spot. We could have a leisurely conversation here. I gave the order for a fresh round of tea, looked at him and said, 'We can talk here.'

'Yes, we can talk peacefully here,' he said, expressing his satisfaction.

'So, what do you think? What will happen now?'

At that very moment, two men entered the room and came and sat down at a table near us. One of them happened to look at the *Supplement* lying on our table. 'So! The *Supplement* has been published,' and with these words, he approached our table and asked, 'Can I see it?'

'Certainly,' I said and handed him the one-page newspaper.

He took the *Supplement*, went to sit at his table with the newspaper spread out before him on it, and began to read it. A gentleman sitting at a table some distance away, too, spotted the open *Supplement*. 'Oh! The *Supplement* has come?' And he walked up to our neighbour's table and, bent over its open page, began to read it. He had announced his discovery in such a loud voice that whoever heard it at the adjacent tables instantly perked up their ears. Several people walked over to the table where the *Supplement* lay face up.

'So what does the *Supplement* say?'

Sermonizing, criticizing, analysing voices, a cautionary tone here, a discordant note there, a comment laced with grief, more debates, sharp tones, and voices raised higher and higher.

The two of us looked on in silence until he spoke up restlessly, 'Yaar, there is too much noise here. It is difficult to sit here and talk.'

'So shall we get out of here?'

And we came out. We had thought Café d'Place would have a more peaceful ambience. But the moment we set foot there, we felt as if we had entered a sea of noise. Then, we looked into several other tea houses. But everywhere, there was the same crush of people, the same noise.

'Yaar, there is too much noise!'

'I cannot understand why everything is so noisy today,' I said.

'And look at the crowds! It looks as though the entire

city has come out to drink tea and gossip. Everyone looks so carefree!'

'So much noise! Such a rush! It is going to be difficult for us to breathe in this city,' I said in agreement.

'Yaar, this city used to be so quiet! How contentedly we used to walk down this road!'

I ran my eyes down the length of the road. Buses, cars, taxis, rickshaws and, most of all, scooters ... there was a veritable storm of traffic! And the noise! ... Dear God! At that moment, when we were in search of a quiet nook, we realized how noisy the city had become and how crowded, too.

Perhaps, by now, the desire to talk had grown strong within him too. He was as eager as I was to find a quiet nook somewhere. How many places we went to and how many times we returned disappointed! And our desire for a peaceful conversation was such that it only became stronger – as though we had to resolve national issues today!

'All the restaurants are full. Let us go to Company Bagh.'[2]

And we left the noisy main road and took a quiet side street. A few more steps brought us to Company Bagh. The very air of the garden was redolent with peace and tranquillity. A few people could be seen here or there; some

---

[2] A sprawling colonial-era garden in Lahore, just off the Mall. Incidentally, the large public garden is not far from Intizar Husain's home on Jail Road. He has, elsewhere in his writings, mentioned going for a daily walk in Company Bagh. According to local Lahori lore, the ubiquitous Club Sandwich, found on the menus of most colonial-era clubhouses across the subcontinent, is said to have been devised by a chef in the club located in the garden premises.

were walking on a footpath; others were sitting quietly on benches. We too sat down on a stone bench. We had crossed a sea of noise; we wanted to rest for a while. A couple passed close by; as they walked ahead, the young man held the girl's hand. They walked in the shade of the trees until they went around a dense tree and disappeared from sight.

'No details are available. There is confusion all around,' he muttered.

'Paani re paani, tera rang kaisa?'[3] the song could be heard from a distance.

The song kept coming closer. A young man, with a transistor slung from one arm, was walking along. He sat down on the patch of grass near us, put down his transistor on one side and began to untie his shoe laces. The song attracted both of us. We listened attentively.

'Is it Lata?'

'Yes. And Kishore Kumar with her,' I said.

But, soon afterwards, the volume of the transistor steadily increased. One more song by Lata, then another, then yet another till a group of raucous young men appeared on the

_____

[3] *'Paani re paani, tera rang kaisa …'* These are the words of a popular song from the Hindi film *Shor* (1972). That it is being played on a transistor radio is an indication of the immense popularity of Hindi cinema on both sides of the border. The extent of knowledge about film trivia is another indication of how widespread this interest is among all sections of Pakistani society. Evidently, young men roaming public gardens listen to Hindi film songs with as much interest as the city's intellectuals. Incidentally, the song is a duet sung by Lata Mangeshkar and Mukesh, not Kishore Kumar as mentioned here.

scene. They too sat down on a patch of grass near us. They had a tape recorder. They began to listen to songs of their choice.

'Yaar, this is the most awful boriyat.'[4]

'And their taste is so atrocious, so vulgar!' I was getting angry at this new lot.

'We will find no haven in this city today.'

'I don't understand why people must listen to songs at such high volumes.'

'The slow tunes have become ineffectual. The noise all around is such that no one can hear what the other has to say. What can one have to say in such a world?'

And we both fell silent. On one side there was the transistor, on the other the tape recorder. Noise on our left, noise on our right. Defeated and depressed, we stood up. We walked along some footpaths. Evening had fallen by now. The crowd of walkers had swollen. We came out of the park.

'We should listen to the BBC,'[5] and with these words, he

---

[4] I wanted to retain this word to introduce English readers to an expression widely used among Urdu speakers. Like several English words that have been adapted and subsequently incorporated into the Urdu lexicon, 'boriyat' retains the original meaning of the English word boredom but also has an extra dash of tedium, ennui and weariness.

[5] Before the advent of 24x7 news channels, across much of South Asia, the British Broadcasting Corporation (BBC) was considered the most trustworthy source of news. The BBC reporters, such as Mark Tully, have been at the forefront of reporting on all major man-made events as well as natural calamities; their bulletins have been beaming

started off. After all, the thought was stuck in his head; if anything, it was pricking him like a thorn. Till the thorn was pulled out, neither of us could rest in peace. The thorn was slowly being pulled out when we heard the sound of footsteps from behind us. The person behind us was approaching with swift strides. We slowed down; soon, he overtook us. Now we could talk in peace, but the road was such that people often came here for their evening walks and the gentleman who was walking behind us was walking in such a leisurely fashion that even when we slackened our pace, we could not reduce the distance between him and us.

'Come, let us go home,' I suggested.

'You live alone, don't you?'

'Yes, of course.'

'Let us go, then; we can talk in peace over there.'

We turned around. I reached home, opened my door and said, 'Sit down.'

As he sat down, he looked around. 'Yaar, don't you have a radio?'

'Neither radio nor transistor.'

'Well, if you had one, we could have listened to the BBC.'

'Do you think the BBC will reveal anything?'

'Of course, it will. Anyway, today, we must listen to our

news on the radio into homes long before the notion of 'breaking news' became common. The BBC could also be relied upon to give a fairly balanced report, often unlike the news that filtered out from state-controlled news agencies. In Pakistan especially, where news would be severely controlled by the military regimes, the BBC could be the only source of independent news.

own radio too. But, anyway, you have not indulged in these entanglements. No radio, no TV.'

'Wives are known to collect such things,' I said.

'And wife and children are an entanglement too.'

'That is why I haven't got any.'

'Good for you; you live in peace.' And then after a moment's pause, 'I think your neighbours are all bachelors too.'

'How can you tell?'

'It is very quiet here, yaar.'

'It is not a mohalla; it is a block of flats. You can't tell in flats, but there are large families living in the apartments on either side.'

I thought, first of all, I should arrange for some tea. One can talk contentedly when there is tea. I looked for milk; it was there. Tea leaves and sugar could usually be found. I filled the kettle with water and put it on the heater.

'Yaar, there seem to be no children in your neighbourhood.'

'No, yaar, there are lots of them.'

'I can't hear them. In fact, there is no sound at all.'

I said, 'This is a flat; don't go by the sounds in a mohalla.'

But my answer did not satisfy him. He spoke after a moment's silence, 'It is very quiet here. It seems as though we have come to a jungle.'

I said nothing. My attention was focussed on the hissing water.

'What are you doing?'

'I am making tea; it will be ready in a minute. Then we can talk at leisure.'

'Let it be, yaar. Let us go back to our usual place and drink tea.' And he got up abruptly, saying: 'This place is making me anxious.'

I looked at him in surprise and said, 'But we can talk peacefully here.'

'All right, but,' and he glanced at the watch strapped to his wrist, 'if we sit here, we will miss the news. Let us go back to our regular place; it has a radio. We can listen to the news.' And, after a moment's respite, he said, 'Sitting here, it seems as though we are cut off from the rest of the world.'

'It is true; once inside this room, my link with the world snaps totally. In here, I do not know what is happening outside. Actually, the room doesn't even have a window from where you can see the sky.' We came out; the road was empty.

'What is the time?' he asked and looked at the watch strapped on his wrist with some alarm. 'How odd! It has become so quiet so early!'

Indeed, it was quiet. There would be some noise whenever a rickshaw passed by, but as soon as it was gone, the silence would intensify. We could hear the sound of our own footsteps. We began to walk slowly. We reached our usual haunt. Today the restaurant had emptied so early! Only a short while ago, we had left it so crowded! At that time you couldn't hear a word. Now, only two men were found seated at a solitary table; soon, they too got up and left. Now we were the only two people. We gave the order for tea.

'This place has become so deserted so early,' he said.

'That is good; we can't talk in a crowd.'

'Yes, it is good,' and then after a minute's thought, he added, 'Yaar, there is a lot of confusion.'

'Was there no confusion before?'

'You are right; there was confusion before too,' and he lapsed into silence. Finally, he spoke again, 'There is no clarity on what can be behind this, but I think …' And he had nearly taken off when the tea arrived. Once again, he fell silent and began to pour his tea. As he was making his cup, he said, 'The girl was nice.'

'Girl? What girl?'

'The girl we saw in Company Bagh.'

'Oh! That one!' And the girl with her youthful bosom and ample derriere floated in both our imaginations.

'Yes. She was nice.'

It was as though a still breeze had given way to a cool burst of fresh air. Or so I felt. He too was looking sprightly. We ran our mind's eye over the outlines of her pleasing body and concluded that the girl was very nice indeed.

'Yaar!' he spoke meditatively, 'Our life is bereft of a girl.'

I laughed and said, 'When did we ever have one?'

'No, really,' he spoke seriously. 'At least there wasn't this desolation before.'

Once again I laughed, but gave no answer.

Then, after some more thought, he asked, 'Did you ever see her?'

I was surprised. 'Who?'

'That one.'

Now I understood who he was asking about. Suddenly saddened, I said, 'No, yaar.'

'You mean, you never saw her again after that?'

'No.'

'That's very strange.'

I too had found it very strange at the time. After having been surprised and sorrowful, I had become free of it. But now that he had expressed his surprise, once again I was experiencing that sense of amazement; she had disappeared so completely that I never saw her again.

'Yaar, you have suffered the same fate as me.'

'The same fate that befalls every decent man,' I added.

And with that, we both became sorrowful. He did not say anything more, nor did I feel like saying another word. We sat in silence and drank our tea. The time for the BBC news came and passed. And then Radio Pakistan, followed by All India Radio. The time for each news bulletin came and went.

'Yaar, should we go?'

'Yes, let us go.'

And we both set off – he towards his house and I towards mine.

Between Me and the Story[1]

That day I picked up the pen with the intention of writing a story. I had sat down with complete concentration. But the television set had been left on. Since I am no TV addict, even popular serials and programmes leave me cold and, ordinarily, I can continue with my reading and writing, unperturbed and unaffected. That day it wasn't so; even though that day there wasn't a particularly riveting serial or a fun and games show on air. In fact, a very serious programme was being aired – a demonstration of national pride. A film on Pakistan's experiments with the atomic bomb was being played. A mighty explosion occurred. The earth rumbled and shook. Then I saw the mountain quiver ever so slightly and its colour began to change imperceptibly, almost like the colour fading from a human face. I put my pen down. Or, perhaps, it stopped writing on its own and I had no other option but to put it down.

---

[1] Published as 'Mere aur Kahani ke Beech' in the short story collection *Sheherzad ke Naam,* Sang-e-Meel Publications, Lahore, 2002.

In my childhood, whenever there was a lunar or solar eclipse, my father would put away all his chores and sit down on the prayer rug. He would offer two prayers, which he called the Prayers of Fear. He would say that a great misfortune had befallen the moon, and we must pray to God that the crisis be averted and the Hour of Reckoning pass without any mishap. Perhaps, at this moment, just such an Hour of Reckoning had approached a mountain in Pakistan. In its moment of trial and tribulation, that mountain showed such amazing grace and strength! It bore the brunt of the havoc and destruction that the explosion brought in its wake and did not allow even a strand of hair to be hurt in Pakistan. How it must have suffered can be gauged from the fact that it quivered and lost its colour when the explosion ripped through it. It would never regain its lost colour.

Until yesterday, the atom bomb had been beyond our reach; it was, after all, a rare and exceptional weapon of mass destruction that could only be the prized possession of superpower armouries from across the seven seas. In the blink of an eye, it had fallen into our hands. Strange, very strange indeed! Now we too are an atomic power. An atomic power is a superpower. And who doesn't want to be a superpower? So now the people of India must be very happy. The people of Pakistan are also very happy. It is the superpowers who are a worried lot now. They had signed countless agreements and counter-agreements among themselves that come what may, they would never use their weapons of mass destruction. Now they are bedevilled by this classic instance of the runaway monkey and the razor;

no one knows who the runaway monkey will slash! What is more, who knows when these two will press the button and annihilate the rest of the world along with themselves?

These days, I remember so many stories I had heard in my childhood from my grandmother. One of the stories was about a down-at-luck prince who gets caught in the snare of a genie. The genie lived in a grand fortress. He took the prince to his fortress and let him loose, saying 'You are free in every way inside this fortress. There are seven doors here. You can open six of them; they will lead you to several amazing delights. You may have your fill of those delights. But do not open the seventh door. If you do, a great calamity will befall you.' The prince followed the genie's advice for many days. Of the six doors, each door lead to a cornucopia of plenty – there was every manner of bounty to suit every taste and delectation. Finally, the prince tired of these gratifications: One day he decided to open the seventh door to find out what great pleasures it hid. And the moment he opened the seventh door, a great calamity fell upon his head.

Our times, too, are caught in a genie's snare – the genie of science and technology. In small countries, we are not fully aware of it. Go to any developed country in the West. Truly it appears as though the genie from Aladdin's lamp has created those magnificent buildings and fortresses. Open any door and you will find such a bewildering array of luxuries and delights that you will be stunned. But a seventh door, too, has appeared in these fortresses. The genie has instructed us to open all other doors, but to always keep the seventh door shut. But sometimes I wonder, what if some eccentric prince were to take it in his head to open the seventh door, what would happen then?

The problem is that this is an age of science and technology, and I still subscribe to ancient tales and the old stories of genies and fairies. My friends tell me that these old yarns are a reminder of mankind's earliest childhood when the human intellect was not fully formed and superstitions reigned supreme. Today, in this age of scientific temper, man depends solely on his wit and intelligence. But I want to know: has the child really grown up? One hears that in the West, he has grown up in the lap of science and philosophy to full adulthood and become a veritable model of intelligence. The atom bomb was crafted by his genius, just as Hiroshima was a spectacular example of his brilliance.

Anyhow, in this age of knowledge when technology is at its zenith, forests and deserts and oceans and mountains and birds and animals are all at risk. My friends say, brother, this is a manifestation of the conquest of nature, and they quote verses by the great poet Iqbal to buttress their theory. I too recall some bits of Iqbal. Two couplets are as follows:

Dhoondnein wala sitaron ki guzargahon ka
Apne afkar ki duniya mein safar kar na saka
Jisne suraj ki shuaon ko giraftar kiya
Zindagi ki shab-e-tareek suhur kar na saka[2]

---

[2] From *'Zamana-e-hazir ka Insan'* in Iqbal's collection *Zarb-i-Kalim*.

(He tracked the orbits of the stars, yet could not
Travel in the world he had created in his thoughts
He captured the rays of the sun, yet could not
Make the sun rise on life's dark night)

If anything, life's dark night has become even darker
since. And it is darkening every day. If there was a ray of
hope left somewhere, that too was snuffed out by the coming
of the atom bomb.

So here I come back to my old song of distress. I have
been singing this song for a very long time. In 1960, when the
magnificently tall peepul tree beside the gate of the Punjab
University was cut down, I felt as though a murder had been
committed in broad daylight and a benign presence lifted
from over our heads. For so long, I had seen eager young
students chitter-chatter in its dense shade. How many stories
lay behind that guileless chit-chat, the tree alone could have
told. But there it lay, face down on the Mall, with the stories
buried forever in its bosom. I used to work for the *Mashriq*[3]
those days. I had turned my face away from politics and wrote
only of small matters concerning people, trees and birds.
So I wrote a column on the martyrdom of the peepul tree
and went to various literary circles pleading its cause. Those
days, progressive and traditionalist writers met at soirees
and discussed all sorts of literary issues. The traditionalists
couldn't understand why the hacking down of a tree was
being presented as a human tragedy and a literary concern.
My progressive friends read my plea as a war between the

---

[3] A newspaper in Karachi, Pakistan

progressives and the regressives. Their argument was that Pakistan is entering an industrial era. So trees will be chopped down. How can the nation progress otherwise?

Soon, trees began to be cut indiscriminately. One day I received a strange phone call. Begum Hijab Imtiaz Ali[4] was on the line: 'Intizar Sahab, are you aware that the koel is silent in the city this year? The month of June has begun, and one hasn't heard the koel coo. Tell me, have you heard it?'

I thought of my morning walks in Jinnah Bagh and remembered with surprise that the season for the koel's calls had begun. But so far I hadn't heard its call, neither from close quarters nor from far away. Why had I not thought about it sooner?

'You are right, madam. I too haven't heard the koel's call so far this season.'

'Then why haven't you written about it in your column? People should know about it. Write about it, Intizar Sahab. Tell people that this is a matter of grave concern. So, will you write then?'

'Yes, I will.'

Truly, this was a matter I should have written about. It made perfect sense to me. After all, some part of the natural world had to protest against the massacre of trees. And the protest came from the koels. They had decided to go silent and thus deprive us of their mellifluous cooing.

---

[4] A prominent fiction writer who wrote old-fashioned romances in Urdu; she was extremely popular, especially among women readers.

The latest issue of *Savera*[5] has just reached me. Salahuddin Mahmood[6] has written in his article that birds, butterflies and fish are committing mass suicide in different parts of the world. Nasir Kazmi[7] had written:

> *Urh gaye yeh shaakh se kah ke tayoor*
> *Is gulistan ki hawa mein zahar hai*

> (The birds have fled from the branches, saying
> There is poison in the air of this garden)

But where will they fly to now? Man has poisoned not just the air in the garden, but the entire world. The birds and the butterflies cannot grasp the hands of foolish, barbaric man and stop him from leaking poison in the air and making life lifeless on the earth that God created. At best, the koels can fall silent in protest. Birds and butterflies can turn despondently away from this foul universe and commit mass suicide. A sensitive butterfly and a twittering bird can give no other answer to man's cruelty and ignorance. They have no deterrent.

But we come back to the same thing: what good is our crying and pleading? We aren't people of any importance. Even Bill Clinton is ignored. No one pays any heed to him. In the atomic fracas between India and Pakistan, American bravado has disappeared in a wisp of smoke. This sea change in the world order is remarkable. In a young Pakistan,

---

[5] A magazine brought out in Lahore, Pakistan

[6] Editor of *Savera*

[7] Prominent Pakistani poet and writer

we had learnt to live in the shadow of two giants, both superpowers, both astonishingly terrifying. Small countries sought refuge from their wrath. If they annoyed one, they would immediately scurry to find a safe haven under the wings of the other. If one frowned with annoyance, the other would rush forward to provide shelter and patronage.

After the collapse of the Soviet Union, the balance of powers was overturned. Anis had written an elegy on the death of Dabeer, both famous elegy-writers: the joy of writing elegies is gone. He was right. Be it poetics or literature, politics or sports, the cricket field or any other field, a virtuoso's real talents are unfurled only when he meets his match. America failed to grasp this truism. But so what? In the past, recalcitrant children would flout the instructions of one grown-up, but submit to another. If they disobeyed one elder, they would obey some other. The practice of obedience, nevertheless, remained intact. But now, only one elder remains. If someone disregards him, who can he be expected to listen to? Children have become headstrong. Their disregard knows no bounds. Earlier, it was the leftist intellectuals who were hell-bent on breaking all the rules. It was a strangely piquant situation. The more headstrong the leftists became, the loftier became the stance of the extreme rightists. American hegemony still remained intact. However, the leftists soon became an endangered species in Pakistan. In fact, the breed seems to have died out since the collapse of the Soviet Union. But how has that helped America? No, if anything, it has harmed American interests. With the fall of communism, the anti-US chant has been picked up by the Maulvi-Mullah brigade. The Maulvi-Mullahs may not have gained the same mileage as leftwing intellectuals, but America has certainly lost out in the bargain. It is no longer the presiding deity it had been for so long.

Anyhow, as I was saying, children have become disobedient. Their irreverence knows no bounds and those who were once the elders are now completely disregarded. In such a scenario, anything can happen now that the atom bomb has fallen in the hands of children.

Only time will tell what will happen next. For now, our heads are raised high with pride. But see, what a firecracker our friend Anwar Sajjad[8] has let off. At a time like this, when the People's Party is trying to remind the people of Pakistan that the credit for acquiring the atom bomb must rightfully go to Bhutto Sahab, Anwar Sajjad has dug up evidence to prove that Manto was actually the first man who dreamt of atomic power for Pakistan. And he has cited Manto's writings in the form of letters to Uncle Sam. Sajjad read his article in a discussion organized by a newspaper and sent a copy to me. I read the article and was consumed by sheer astonishment that Manto had had such a dream! According to Anwar Sajjad, Manto's dream simply awaited a man of action who would make it come true. This vision eventually took the form of Zulfiqar Ali Bhutto who was instrumental in giving it a concrete shape.

I read Manto's letters to Uncle Sam a second time. Once

---

[8] Pakistani writer of modern, abstract short stories

again, I was lost in amazement. This time, I was perplexed
more by Anwar Sajjad than the letters. There was a world
of difference between what Manto had written and the
meaning Anwar Sajjad had derived from it. Manto never
wrote the Anwar Sajjad brand of abstract short stories where
anyone can ascribe any meaning he or she wants. Manto
has a fairly straightforward satire. He asks Uncle Sam why
the hydrogen bomb is being prepared. Which countries are
going to be wiped off the surface of the earth? And if that
is the plan, how about giving a small atom bomb to the
favourite nephew who is sick and tired of those fellows from
across the border who don't believe in washing their butts?
Why not just get rid of them once and for all?

This reminds me of a Bombay film called *Eight Days*,
made shortly before Partition. Manto had acted in the film
and probably also written its script. He had enacted the role
of a halfwit who goes around with a ball in his hand, which
he calls an atom bomb, and scares everyone by threatening
to hurl it. The thought of the film scares me. But then, I am
a coward. These days, the people of Asia are under the spell
of the atom bomb. Some are worried about its long-term
consequences, but many others are delighted at the magical
wand that has fallen into their hands. The atom bomb has
had different effects on different people. Its effect on me
is that I cannot write a story any more. On Anwar Sajjad,
the effect has been totally different. Strange, very strange
indeed. First he saluted the Marxist revolution, then became
a fervent devotee of the Islamic bomb. In his article, he
has appealed to the Muslim community that now that we

have become an atomic power, we must strive to become an Islamic superpower.

May the revolution bring happiness to the Believers!

Consider this: even in this new world order, Anwar Sajjad has found a mission for himself. And I, I have once again been left behind. I can see no other mission but the modest one of writing a story. And my story, too, is surrounded by afflictions. Whenever I pick up my pen, the mountain of Chaghai comes and stands before my eyes. First a slight rumble shivers through it, then its colour begins to fade. After every little while, a sound emerges which causes panic among the people. The entire city lives in the thrall of this Mountain of Summons.[9] No other sound reaches here. Suddenly, the mountain loses all colour. Its effect on me is like the call from the Mountain of Summons. The magic of the atom bomb does not work on me. I live in the tormented shadow of that mountain. I can write my story only if I am able to overcome its paralysing fear. But this pain-riddled mountain has come and stood between the story and me.

---

[9] Kuh-e-Nida, meaning the Mountain of Summons. The legendary mount from which the call of death comes from the other world.

The Death of Sheherzad[1]

Sheherzad told over a thousand stories and gave birth to three sons in a thousand and one nights. The listener prospered and so did the teller. The teller of the stories, Sheherzad, was granted life through her stories and, in turn, allowed countless virgins to live, virgins who would have been queen for a night and had their heads lopped off in the morning. The listeners, Duniyazad and the emperor Shaharyar, had their lives changed irrevocably by the stories. The ill will Shaharyar had borne towards all womankind was washed away by Sheherzad's stories. He renounced his practice of marrying a girl for a night and having her head chopped off the next morning.

There was great rejoicing in the kingdom. The capital was bedecked and a grand feast organized. But Sheherzad was in such a state of befuddlement that she continued to look askance at the change in her situation. How could she forget those thousand and one nights when she had told her stories

---

[1] Published as 'Sheherzad ki Maut' in the short story collection *Sheherzad ke Naam,* Sang-e-Meel Publications, Lahore, 2002.

under the cloud of death? And when she began to accept that those nights were truly in the past, a great amazement overtook her. She could hardly believe that she had kept such a long vigil and spent so many sleepless nights, and spun such yarns that had caught the emperor's fancy. How had she drummed up so many fables? They must have come from up above, through God's Grace.

Finally, she could contain herself no longer. One night, she made Duniyazad sit beside her and said, 'Dear sister, now when I think about it, my mind clouds over. I spent a thousand and one nights telling stories! Tell me, how did it happen?'

Duniyazad answered, 'Sister, I myself am amazed that you had such a treasure trove of stories buried in your memory. Those nights were terrifying. My heart would beat with terror at what the new dawn would bring. I could see Death hovering close, always close by. But those dark and fearful nights were lit up, as though by lamps, by the stories you told. Once you started telling your stories, one never knew how much time passed and when the night slipped past. And the emperor ... he would sit spellbound, listening to your tales.'

Sheherzad said, 'Sister, I was lost to the world. All I could think of was that I *had* to tell a story and save my life each night. But once I began, I would get so engrossed in it that all thoughts of staying alive would recede. Then, the only thought that spurred me on was that I must bring my story to its conclusion.'

'Your story did reach its conclusion. And what a

conclusion! By the end of it, the emperor was a transformed man. From a misogynist who had a woman's head axed every morning to a husband who is devoted to you – he is a new man!'

And the two sisters relived those nights of terror and uncertainty, and wept. Then they wiped their tears and offered thanksgiving to the Lord for ending their misfortune. God had given Sheherzad the strength and wisdom to tell those stories, the stories that helped save their lives.

Talking to her sister and sharing her sadness and fear made Sheherzad feel better. Soon, the festivities wound down. The kingdom slowly returned to normal and things continued as before. The thousand and one nights became a thing of the past. Sheherzad, as the Emperor Shaharyar's favourite wife and the mother of three charming princes, reigned over the harem. Duniyazad decided to forsake marriage and motherhood and live in her sister's shadow.

Sheherzad's sons grew up. They were married with great pomp and festivity. Maidens as beautiful as the moon entered the palace as their brides. In due course, the wombs of each were blessed and flower-like little girls were born to them. As the girls grew up, Duniyazad noticed that they were more interested in listening to stories than in fun and games. She said to them, 'Girls, if you are so interested in stories, get your grandmother to tell you some. There is no one in the whole wide world who can match her when it comes to storytelling.'

Upon hearing this, the three girls went to Sheherzad and insisted that she tell them stories. Sheherzad was taken aback at the children's insistence. She had forgotten that once upon a time she had been a great teller of tales. She tried her best to dissuade her granddaughters, but the girls wouldn't budge. Duniyazad reproached her sister, 'Dear sister, I know it is not my place to speak between a grandmother and her granddaughters, but justice demands that I speak up. These girls are, after all, your granddaughters. They have a grandmother sitting at home who is a storyteller par excellence. Why then should these poor things be bereft of your great gift? Why should they go knocking on other people's doors to hear stories?'

Sheherzad's heart melted at her sister's words. She said to her granddaughters, 'My darlings, of course I will tell you stories; if not you, who will I tell stories to? But it is daytime now, and stories told in the day cause wayfarers to lose their way. Wait for the night, then I will tell you stories.'

How they waited for the night! As night fell, the three granddaughters surrounded their grandmother. Duniyazad came too. She would be listening to one of Sheherzad's stories after such a long time.

But a strange thing happened. Sheherzad thought hard, racked her brains, tried desperately to remember a story, but she drew a blank. She couldn't remember even one tale. Worried, she said to Duniyazad, 'My memory has fogged over. I can't remember a single story!'

'What a thing to say!' Duniyazad exclaimed. 'You told so many stories to your husband. Why don't you tell any one of them to these girls?'

'But which one? I can't seem to remember even one.'

'What about the one you told on the very first night ... the one about the merchant and the genie.'

'The story of the merchant and the genie ...' Sheherzad muttered.

She tried hard to recollect it. When she couldn't remember a thing, she grew alarmed and said, 'Duniyazad, I can't recall what happened in the story about the merchant and the genie.'

'You mean you have forgotten your own story? Don't you remember ... the merchant ate the date and spat out the stone, and the moment he spat the stone, a great cloud of mist arose and a genie appeared. The genie thundered that the merchant's stone had hit his son in the chest and he had died on the spot. The genie swore, "I will make you pay. Be prepared to die!"'

Sheherzad listened attentively. She tried hard to remember what had happened next, but when nothing emerged from the haze of her mind, she said, 'My dear sister, Duniyazad, I seem to have clean forgotten the story, but you have it at your fingertips. Why don't *you* tell the story to the girls?'

Duniyazad thought for a moment, then said, 'You are the Nightingale of a Thousand and One Tales. I can't match the magic you can create in your storytelling. If you insist, I can tell the story now in my rough-and-ready fashion, but on the condition that tomorrow you will tell the next story in your own inimitable style.'

Sheherzad agreed to her sister's condition. And Duniyazad told the story of the merchant and the genie with great relish to the three little girls. The girls were delighted.

Duniyazad said, 'Girls, my tongue does not have the magic of Sheherzad's. Tomorrow, when your grandmother tells you the next story, you will enjoy it much more.'

A great tumult arose in Sheherzad's mind after listening to Duniyazad's tale. All the tales she had told in the past rose up in great swarms in the coils of her memory, but not one story was complete. Bits and pieces of stories swirled and eddied in the recesses of her mind. Well, never mind, Sheherzad consoled herself. At least my memory has been jogged. Tomorrow, when I sit down to tell a story, God willing, all will be well. I will remember the whole story.

And so the following night, she sat down with her granddaughters with complete assurance. Duniyazad, too, came and sat close beside her. But all that Sheherzad could recall was that the next story she had told Shaharyar had been about the fisherman and the genie. Beyond that, she couldn't remember a thing. Duniyazad prompted, 'Sister, once upon a time, a fisherman cast his net in a river. When the net grew heavy, he thought he had caught a big, fat fish. But when he pulled out the net, he found a sealed brass pot caught in it. The seal belonged to King Solomon. When he broke the seal and opened the pot, a dense black cloud engulfed the day and turned it into night. Out of that black cloud came an immensely tall and huge genie.'

Sheherzad spoke wonderingly, 'It seems to me, Duniyazad, that you will do a better job telling this story as you remember it so well. You might as well tell the rest of the story since I can't recall what happens next!'

With God's grace, Duniyazad was in full flow and fine

fettle. She began the story of the fisherman and the genie with all of Sheherzad's aplomb and by morning had told the entire story. Sheherzad heard Duniyazad's story as though it were her sister's creation, and not her own. She was among the listeners now. And the three little girls were absolutely entranced.

The following night, Sheherzad was confident that she would remember the third story in the chain. When she couldn't remember that particular story, she tried to recollect some other. She managed to drum up the one about Aladdin and the magic lamp, but in that too, she couldn't quite get the chain of events right. Again, Duniyazad had to be called to tell the story.

Now Sheherzad was like a woman possessed. She would try feverishly to recollect the stories she had once told with such elan. But nothing would rise from the fog of oblivion. At her request, Duniyazad would tell the stories till, one by one, all the stories were told.

Sheherzad heard the stories with great wonder. Did I tell all these stories? she thought in amazement.

Gradually, the surprise was replaced by sadness. She had told these stories over a thousand and one nights. And during those thousand and one nights, she had thought each night would be her last one. But now, after all these years, she felt those nights had been the sum total of her life. They spread over her being like a magic spell. I had been fully alive only on those nights, she thought ruefully. Once again, those forgotten, dormant nights rose up and swirled around her. As the night progressed, she wandered far and wide – across unknown islands, oceans and deserts – with the characters that had once peopled her stories. She strayed so far in her ramblings that all the fears and apprehensions of life and death were left far, far behind. And when day had broken and the cock crowed to herald a new dawn, the certitude with which she postponed the story to the following night had made Death take a timorous step back.

Sheherzad remained lost in the enchantment of those story-filled nights. And when she emerged from the trance into the darkness of her present and its empty nights, she thought, 'Now my nights are desolate. They are only long and dark. The magic has fled from them. They have become barren.' She sighed and sank into a deep sadness.

When the emperor came to the harem, he found Sheherzad unnaturally quiet. Despondency dripped from her face. He kept quiet that day, but when he saw that her state was not getting any better and she remained steeped in sorrow, he grew anxious. Finally, he could contain himself no longer and asked, 'I have noticed for many days now that you no longer sparkle with happiness. You don't smile, or talk. Your face looks drawn and pale and sad. What is the matter with you? What is it that is gnawing away at you?'

On hearing these words, Sheherzad abandoned all attempts at restraint and composure. She wept and said, 'O dear husband, which Sheherzad are you referring to? The chirping, chattering, storytelling Sheherzad who entered your palace died a long time ago.'

The emperor was astounded by these words. Perplexed,

he said, 'What is this I hear? If something is weighing on your heart, there must be some reason for it.'

'O my emperor and dear husband,' Sheherzad spoke in a tearful voice, 'you granted me life but snatched away my stories from me. I lived only in my stories. When my stories ended, my own story ended with them.'

Dream and Reality[1]

❧

Mounted on our camels, we held our breath and rode in utter silence along the track till Abu Tahir reined in his mount and announced in a tone of quiet contentment: 'We have come away.'

'Come away?' The three of us looked at Abu Tahir in astonishment and disbelief. 'Friend, can we trust your word?'

Abu Tahir answered with complete conviction, 'I swear by He who has control over my life. We have come out of the City of the Unfaithful.'

Still we deliberated. We looked all around us with our eyes wide and minutely examined our surroundings. The known and familiar buildings of Kufa were no longer visible. This was a new landscape. It was then that we realized we had really come away. We got off our mounts and almost without our volition fell down in prostration and gave thanks to He who gave life to us. Then we sat in the shade of the palm trees that grew beside the track and opened our parcels of

---

[1] Published as 'Khwaab aur Haqeeqat' in *Intizar Husain aur Un ke Afsane,* Educational Book House, Aligarh.

food. We gulped a handful of parched gram and drank some water. How cool and sweet the water seemed to us then. It felt as though we had been thirsting for water and had slaked our dry throats after ages. As God is our witness, we had nearly lost all savour and relish in food in that benighted city and even cool, sweet wells had become brackish. Or, perhaps, we had become so devoid of zest that God's bounty had turned tasteless for us.

All this had come about since that person's appearance. Riding a high horse, clad in black robes, his face muffled by a cloth, a sword and shield tied to his waist, he had entered the city. People had thought Imam Zaman, the Leader of the Time, had appeared in their midst. The news spread like wildfire in the lanes and alleys of the city. The people were delighted. The thought of a messiah who would lead them mesmerized them. 'Bravo! Bravo!' they cried and stood in a ring around him. Then they moved in a procession with great fanfare towards the Qasr-ul-Amara, the Grand Palace. It appeared as though the entire city had gushed out and gathered here.

Upon reaching the lofty gates of the palace, he reined in his horse and turned towards the crowd. As he turned, he uncovered his face. With a ferocious expression, spit gathering at the corners of his mouth, he unsheathed his sword and thundered at the crowd, 'Listen, you people, those among you who know already know this, but those who don't know – know that I have come.' A silence fell on the crowd. Those who knew and could see who had come among them and those who saw but did not know who it was – both groups were dumbstruck.

He made his announcement and entered the palace. The crowd stood motionless for a long time until, finally, Abu al-Manzar broke the spell. His tone was one of sadness. 'May the Lord have mercy on the city of Kufa. We had waited so long for someone to appear, and look who has shown up!'

'But who is he who has appeared?'

'Shame on you that you fail to recognize whose son he is! He was born to a slave girl and has no father.'

'The son of Ziyad!'[2] the exclamation broke from someone's lips and then silence descended on the crowd once more.

The news of his coming spread far and wide. Streets and gardens fell empty and quiet. I, Mansur bin Noman al-Hadeedi, had gone through bustling streets and alleys to reach the palace, but now I crossed empty parks and echoing streets to reach my home. And when morning came after a restless night, I left my house and found the city had changed. As God is my witness, I had once seen this city look like a boiling cauldron over a roaring fire, but now I found it as

---

[2] Ubayd Allah ibn Ziyad was the son of Ziyad ibn Abu Sufyan. After his father's death in 673, Ubayd became the Governor of Kufa and Basra. He is an especially despised figure in the history of Islam for his role in the slaying of Husain, the grandson of the Prophet and the son of Ali, in the historic Battle of Karbala on the tenth day of Muharram, in the year 680. In this story, a fictionalized recreation of a historical occurrence involving real-life personages from the early history of Islam, the city of Kufa becomes a metaphor for the great calamities that can befall a people who adopt indifference. The people of Kufa have, on various occasions, functioned as metaphors for hypocrites or those who chose not to speak up against injustice and misuse.

cold as the hearts of those who lust after others. In my heart, I cried over the fanfare with which cities are raised and how quickly they decline.

Heartbroken, I reached the house of my old friend, Mas'ab Ibn-e-Bashir. Tearfully I said, 'O Mas'ab, have you seen how much Kufa has changed in the blink of an eye?'

Mas'ab looked hard at me and said, 'Don't be surprised, Mansur, and speak softly.'

I looked askance at him and said, 'Aren't you the same man who, until yesterday, spoke in a loud voice?'

He said, 'Yesterday Abu al-Manzar spoke the loudest and today he lies dead beneath the walls of the palace.'

And so saying, he quickly took my leave and went towards the palace. Then I knew that Kufa had truly changed and I really ought to have spoken softly. Rather I should not have spoken at all.

I saw how Qais-bin-Mashar had spoken and then fallen silent forever. Ibn-e-Ziyad's men had dragged him to the roof of the palace, saying, 'What do you have to tell?'

In a loud voice, he had made his announcement, an announcement that was heard in every home in this silent city. The very next moment he was pushed off the roof. How long he had sobbed beneath the walls of the palace! After a long time, his friend Abdul Momin bin-Amir came by that way, took out his dagger and drew it across his throat. An old man whispered in his ear, 'A fine way you have of honouring your friendship!' In reply he said, 'I could not bear to see my dear friend sobbing like that.'

I saw this sight and turned away. Troubled, I wandered

among parks and gardens. I felt I was no longer in Kufa, but in some wasteland of fear and terror.

As I wandered in this desolate landscape of terror, I met Abu Tahir. He introduced me to Jafar Raba'ii and Haroon-bin-Sohail. For days, the four of us wandered about that city of fear as though we were deaf and dumb. Finally we let go of the mantle of patience, sat down to talk among ourselves and decided that somehow we must leave this place and go away. Jafar Raba'ii cried when he heard this suggestion. He said, 'I am of the soil of Kufa. How can I leave this soil?'

Haroon-bin-Sohail said, 'Even though I belong to the soil of Medina, I swear upon those who reared me, leaving *this* land will no doubt make me cry too, for I have spent the best years of my youth among these streets and alleys.'

Then Abu Tahir, who was the eldest among us, looked towards me and said, 'What do you have to say about this, O Mansur?'

I offered, 'Friends, remember the hadith of the Prophet: When your city becomes narrow and small for you, you must leave it and go away.'

Upon hearing these words, all three friends were convinced and we began to make preparations for our departure.

How easy we had thought it would be to leave the city, and how difficult it turned out to be.

There were guards at the gates. Those who wished to enter and those who left were barred and questioned. Several times we reached the two gates and quietly returned upon seeing the alert, watchful sentries. Kufa was increasingly becoming cramped and intolerable for us, so cramped that it seemed like a mousetrap. And trapped inside it, we were like the mice that go round and round but are unable to escape.

Seeing no means for our departure, we became utterly despondent. Haroon-bin-Sohail heaved a deep sigh and said, 'If only our mothers had turned barren and our fathers' seed gone to waste so that we would never have been born and never have had to see such black days!'

Jafar Raba'ii cried and said, 'Shame on us that we are willing to endure captivity in our own city and shame on the city too that she has become a stepmother to her own sons.'

Having reached this nadir of despair, we became fearless. After all, what did we have to lose? Somehow we strengthened our resolve and set out. We do not know how it happened. Either the sentries were temporarily blinded or perchance they fell asleep. Be that as it may, we were now out of the city and breathing the air of freedom.

The evening shadows were lengthening and the hot air was turning cooler.

'Friends! The night is dark and the journey is long.'

'Is this night darker than the days we have seen in Kufa?'

The argument went down well with everyone. We agreed to travel on into the ink-black night.

'But where shall we go?'

The question caught everyone unawares. We had simply set out. We had given no thought at all to where we would go.

Abu Tahir thought for a moment, then said, 'Medina, where else?'

Jafar Raba'ii and I agreed with the suggestion, but Haroon-bin-Sohail fell into deep thought. Then, softly, he said, 'What if Medina too has become Kufa?'

All of us looked angrily at him. 'O friend,' Jafar Raba'ii said, 'how can you say such a thing about that resplendent city, especially when you yourself are from its soil?'

Haroon-bin-Sohail checked himself, then said, 'Friends, no doubt it is a holy city. Its soil is fragrant, its water is sacred, but I have met those who have come from it. I have seen how worried they have been.'

At this, we fell silent. No one could think of an answer. But Haroon-bin-Sohail had still not finished. He spoke thoughtfully, 'Friends, the more I think about it, the more it surprises me that the cities that were once lit by the Light of Truth turned over to the other side so quickly. How quickly their days became disconsolate and their nights without rest!'

Abu Tahir looked angrily towards him and said, 'O disobedient, untrue son of Sohail, may your mother sit in mourning over you! Do you refute the essential Truth of Islam?'

Haroon-bin-Sohail said, 'Respected Elder, I seek shelter from the day when I may inadvertently cast doubt on the wisdom of my elders and refute the Truth that is Islam, but Kufa …'

Abu Tahir cut him off angrily, 'What about Kufa? What do you want to say?'

'That is exactly what I am trying to say: what is it about Kufa and why? The more I push away all thoughts of Kufa, the more they crowd around me. Why does Kufa appear in the midst of thoughts of that holy city? And why does it appear so quickly? It hasn't even been very long since the hijrat of the Prophet.'

I could see Abu Tahir's temper rising. I decided to intervene. 'My suggestion is that we proceed towards that city which has been called by the highest of the highs the City of Peace. Even if the world is run over by tyrants and the earth is carpeted in riots, there will be no disorder in the peace and tranquillity of the holy city of Mecca.'

Everyone agreed with my suggestion, and we mounted our camels immediately. The darkness was immense, for this was one of those nights that fall in the early days of the new moon. But our resolve drew us inexorably on. The night became steadily drenched with dew and the nip in the air filled our hearts with delight. Engrossed in thoughts of the City of Peace, drunk on the heady brew of freedom, we rode on. I nearly dozed off on my camel and what a beautiful dream I saw! I was sitting in the City of Peace amidst pious and saintly elders, telling them about the state of affairs in Kufa when, suddenly, I heard a voice. 'But we have once again reached there.' Startled, I opened my eyes. It was dawn and before us lay the walls of Kufa.

'We have once again reached here,' Jafar Raba'ii was speaking.

Abu Tahir and Haroon-bin-Sohail looked at the walls, their eyes filled with astonishment and terror.

'But how is that possible?' The words escaped my mouth.

Abu Tahir took a minute to think. Then he said, 'The night was exceedingly dark. We did not pay attention to the direction we were taking. We took the same path we had taken to escape.'

We were all silent.

'What shall we do now?' Jafar Raba'ii asked.

Once again, Abu Tahir weighed his words carefully, then said, 'It is impossible to go back, for the guards have spotted us. Perhaps Nature does not want us to leave this place.'

Haroon bin-Sohail took a long, shuddering breath and said, 'You are right. Kufa is our destiny.'

And I, Mansur bin Noman al-Hadeedi, became sorrowful and said, 'Yes, Mecca is our dream; Kufa is our fate.'

And we trooped back into Kufa, tired and defeated.

The Story about the Monkeys of the Big Forest[1]

This is the tragic tale of the monkeys of the Big Forest, the monkeys that have since disappeared without a trace. The place where the monkeys once lived has turned into a city full of human beings; where there were once tall trees there are now sky-scraping buildings. It is said that once upon a time there was a densely forested tract here. There were monkeys on the trees, so many monkeys that they could scarcely be counted. The monkeys had sharp teeth, sharper claws and strong bodies. Their life was all about ravaging and pillaging the groves and orchards far and near, lunging from the branch of one dense tree to the other and eating the ripe and unripe fruits that grew on them. The monkeys were

[1] Published as 'Mahaban ke Bandaron ka Qissa' in *Shaharzad ke Naam*, Sang-e-Meel Publications, Lahore, 2002. I have used the expression Big Forest for Mahaban, which is a generic term in Hindi for any dense or big forest, a bit like Roopnagar in the story entitled 'Circle'. This propensity to use a common noun as a proper noun is typical of Intizar Husain.

free-spirited and fearless. They spent their days jumping from tree to tree in the dense undergrowth, climbing the highest branches of the tallest trees to touch the skies and outdoing each other in jumping higher and further.

Those who tended the orchards and the fields were heartily sick of the monkeys. The monkeys were known to be so ferocious that those who tended the orchards and the fields did not have the courage to face them. Once, a wise farmer came up with a novel scheme. He brought some gram, a big chunk of jaggary and some sticks, and placed them under a large tree in the Big Forest. He came back and told the owners of the orchards and the fields that henceforth their crops would be safe and the wayfarers would be able to travel safely through the forest because he had taken care of the monkey menace.

The monkeys saw the gram and the chunk of jaggary and came down from the trees and fell upon the gram. The gram, at least, they shared among themselves, but one greedy monkey grabbed the chunk of jaggary and went off to eat it by himself. An alert monkey saw this and immediately leapt towards the greedy monkey, grabbed the jaggary and went off to a far side. A sturdy monkey saw this and pounced to grab the jaggary and made off with it. The other monkeys saw the jaggary disappearing before their eyes and fell upon their fleeing comrade. Soon, the chunk of jaggary was up for grabs – now in one pair of paws, now in another. In the midst of this melee, one monkey got a strange idea in his head; he picked up one of the sticks and brought it down hard on the head of the monkey who held the chunk of jaggary. The monkey's head split wide open and the chunk of jaggary fell from his clutches. The monkey with the stick immediately pounced on the jaggary. At first, the pack of monkeys stood in fearful stillness at this strange sight, but then they saw more sticks lying under the tree. The sturdier among them picked up a stick each. The fight that now broke out among them cannot be described. One suffered a broken head, another a broken leg, still another a bloodied mouth.

When the monkeys were exhausted and paused to draw a breath, they went and sat down far away from each other. That is when they saw that the oldest among them was sitting on a high branch of a peepal tree; his eyes were closed and his head was bent. The old monkey was the wisest in their community. All the other monkeys respected him. Seeing him sitting with his eyes closed and head bent, they crowded around him, enquiring about his health and asking why he sat in such a manner. The wise old monkey raised his head to look at them with his red eyes and, speaking in a sorrowful voice, mourned the plummeting standards of social etiquette among monkeys, their fall into the pit of human-ness, and the fact that their unity was being ripped to shreds.

The words of the wise monkey had a deep impact on the other monkeys. The next day, they did not fight amongst themselves at all. When the wise farmer came to place the gram and jaggary under the tree once more, those monkeys who had picked up sticks took possession of the goods. They distributed them among all the monkeys. The other monkeys were happy: they didn't get their heads bashed up and yet got to eat the gram and jaggary.

The wise farmer turned out to be a canny man: every day he would deposit a lot of gram and jaggary under the tree. The monkeys thought it was a good thing they got their daily sustenance without having to forage and plunder orchards and fields. But monkey business, as you know, is famous for a good reason. Some days one monkey would get a larger share and some days an especially good-looking female monkey would get a bigger share than the others. This would cause an outcry among the monkeys who would climb the branches of the trees and let loose a raucous protest. Sometimes, one monkey would clatter its teeth and get into a scuffle with another. They would fight and grapple with each other, but then, after some time, peace would be restored.

Once, it so happened that the gram fell short. The monkeys screeched and howled at each other. One monkey climbed down from his perch on the high branches of a tree and created such a din that his face grew red as a burning ember. But soon, like the others, he was exhausted and fell silent. The next day, the gram fell shorter still, and it so happened that while some monkeys stuffed their faces with the gram, others could get no more than a few grains. On the third day, a matter of minutes after they had been placed under the tree, only the gram remained and the chunk of jaggary disappeared. No one knew who had picked it up or where it had been hidden. Soon, it became a matter of routine: the chunk of jaggary would disappear in the blink of an eye, and the gram fell to the lot of some while most had to do without any. In the early days, this would cause great outrage among the monkeys and they would let loose a clamour, but soon their anger abated. Unfortunately, they had completely abandoned their practice of pillaging and ravaging orchards and fields. They were completely focussed on the jaggary and gram that was left for them every day.

One fine day, the monkeys created an uproar when they could get no gram. A young monkey appeared among them, propped himself against the trunk of a tree and launched into a speech on the impermanence of gram. This was an entirely new move for the others. They looked at this self-appointed spokesperson with wide-open eyes. When they could not understand what was going on, they closed their eyes. One of them began to pick the lice out of his female's head. A young female climbed a tree and hung upside down from a branch. When the young monkey finished his speech, the wise old monkey looked closely at him and announced in a sorrowful tone: 'This monkey wants to become human.'

This announcement created a furore among the assembled monkeys. They looked closely at the self-appointed monkey, but they could not understand how he could have become human. The self-appointed monkey furiously replied, 'This is a completely false allegation against me.'

The wise monkey said, 'Monkeys are supposed to eat gram, not give speeches on it. If such a thing happens, let it be known that the monkey race has fallen into decline. Evidently, some members of this race want to change their form.'

The monkeys asked, 'O Wise One, what is meant by changing one's form?'

The wise monkey replied, 'When a monkey acquires the traits of another race and, for the sake of this mortal life, changes his way of life, that is known as changing one's form. Have you not heard the story about a monkey named Jan-e Alam?'

The monkeys expressed their surprise and asked, 'Who was Jan-e Alam and what is his story?'

The wise monkey told them, 'It cannot be said with any certainty as to who Jan-e Alam was. I have heard from older monkeys that he was a monkey like us, but had changed his form and become a human. But it has also been said that he was a human who had changed form and become a monkey. Be that as it may, monkeys and humans have always changed and interchanged forms to become one or the other. Sometimes humans become monkeys and sometimes it is the other way round. From my ancestors, I have heard that there was a time when there was a large-scale slaughter of monkeys. Monkey blood became cheaper than the blood of humans. It was in the midst of this calamity that Jan-e Alam was caught and paraded atop an elephant so that the populace could get a good look at him before he was slaughtered. Jan-e Alam came up with a clever idea: he launched into a lecture.

'Three old monkeys, who had somehow managed to evade the vigilant eye of the minister's sons, sat hidden on the branches of a tall tree. As soon as the procession came close by, they peered through the foliage and what do they see? They see a monkey riding atop an elephant. What is more, he is reciting an elegy on the declining world and the sorrowful times in Urdu, and the people around him are scratching their heads in befuddlement.

'One of the three monkeys said in a tone of part-surprise and part-grief, "This creature of God appears to be changing his form. He is talking exactly like a human."

'The second monkey drew a long breath and said, "These are nothing but signs of the decline of the monkey race."

'The third monkey spoke in a tone laced with anxiety, "If this lad continues to exhibit these symptoms, he will ruin our youth."

'The first one spoke in a disappointed tone, "He is hardly likely to return amongst us. He has learnt the use of alliterations in his statements. He will become a teacher at some college amongst humans. He will teach literature or conduct research on the *Fasana-e-Ajaib*."[2]

'The second monkey sighed again and said, "Bad monkeys meet with a bad end."'

And with this, the wise monkey closed his eyes.

The assembly of monkeys was much impressed by this story. But the young monkey addressed the wise one thus, 'O Wise Monkey, one has to be educated to become a teacher, and in order to be educated one has to study books. If monkeys cannot read books, how can they become teachers and how can they teach language and literature?'

The wise monkey looked closely at him and said, 'O Young One, did you not get your gram today …?'

The young monkey replied, 'I haven't got any gram for the past three days.'

---

[2] The *Fasana-e-Ajaib*, written by Mirza Rajab Ali Beg Surur, is one of the most popular dastans in Urdu.

The wise monkey said, 'No wonder you are asking such a question. If monkeys don't get gram to eat they start asking questions. O Child of a Monkey, it is not necessary to be literate to become a teacher, or to have read and studied to be called a learned being. Have you not heard the story of the literate monkey in the qissa of *Alif Laila*?'[3]

The young monkey asked in surprise, 'O Old One, what is the story of the literate monkey in *Alif Laila*?'

Then the wise monkey said, 'The story of the literate monkey in *Alif Laila* goes like this: Once there was a ship that could not reach the shore. When the ship's captain could find no fault with the ship, he addressed his passengers thus, "Friends, there is one among you who has escaped from his master. All of you must write down your name and address, and the one who fails to do so will be deemed the suspicious one and will be taken off the ship." All the passengers wrote down their names and addresses with alacrity. The captain ran his eye over the list, then counted the passengers and found the numbers to be correct. Then he ran his eye over the entire ship and espied a monkey sitting in one corner. He saw the monkey and was alarmed. He immediately decided that the monkey must be taken off the ship.

'The monkey was upset by this decision and, like a human, began to beg and plead. When his entreaties had no effect, he lunged and picked up a pen and wrote down his name and address. Upon seeing this, the people of the ship

---

[3] Refers to the stories contained in the Arabic work of fiction better known as *The Arabian Nights*.

were much amazed and began to exclaim that even monkeys had become people of the pen!

'Then the monkey narrated his tale of sorrows thus: "Friends, I am a monkey of the poet laureate of your city. He raised me since I was a baby. He used to love me dearly. When he sat down to write a qasidah, I would jump into his lap and watch him closely as he wrote and whenever he went out, I would pick up his pen and try to write like him. One day he saw me writing. He saw that the qasidah written by me was much better than his. This made him envious and he ran to kill me. I ran for my life and jumped onto your ship in the hope that I could travel to another city where art would be appreciated and become a source of livelihood for me."

'A physician, who was also a writer, happened to be travelling on the ship. He heard the story and spoke in a sorrowful tone, "Now monkeys too have become people of the pen! Where is the joy of writing?" And so saying, he broke his own pen into pieces and flung them into the sea.'

The wise monkey had narrated this incident to strike awe and terror into the heart of his audience, but since it was the time of the decline of the monkey race, and every instruction has the opposite effect during an age of decline, this strange anecdote had the opposite effect on the young monkey, so much so that he began to dream of turning into Jan-e Alam. And he asked, 'So what happened to Jan-e Alam?'

'Jan-e Alam the monkey turned into Prince Jan-e Alam,' the wise monkey told him.

'How did he suddenly turn from a monkey into a prince?' For a long time, the young monkey mulled over the wise monkey's answer and tried to visualize how Jan-e Alam would have changed form from a monkey to a prince. And he memorized the entire speech that Jan-e Alam had delivered from atop the elephant about the fickle, deceitful world and understood all its intricacies of wordplay. He would climb the highest branch of a tree and, standing on two feet, begin reciting Jan-e Alam's elegantly worded speech: 'This world of changing colours and double-faced people is a place for invoking awe and horror. It is the cause of a thousand sorrows that even the skies favour the wicked. As a result, a monkey becomes a human and a human becomes a monkey. Everyone is helpless before God's will. It is the same for oppression and domination. Wherever you look, no one is free. Everyone is entangled in some problem or the other. Such is His command that even a tongueless nonentity such as me has been granted the gift of such eloquence. He has listed you among the listeners. The world is an old whore. Till yesterday, we monkeys jumped from branch to branch and plucked fruits from the high trees. Now our arms are feeble, our claws have worn out, our teeth are like blunt knives. We live on the jaggary and gram given to us by man. Everyone is a buyer of worldly but transient commodities. No one stops to think what they are buying or selling.'

The other monkeys would listen to this speech in open-mouthed wonder. Then they would laugh loudly and call him a human copy. But the wise monkey would look at him with alarm. He would look at the monkey's back and tail where the hair was receding and his tail was getting rubbed to half its size. And the truth is that the tails of all the monkeys were getting smaller and the hair on their backs was shedding. Their claws had become dull and their teeth had become so loose that even when they tried to close their mouth, their teeth would not stop clattering and they found it difficult to chew gram. The wise monkey would look at them and think, 'O Master of the Monkeys, will the monkey become so debased that he will turn into a tail-less two-legged creature? Will the monkey race that had once spun stories of monkey-hood in groves and forests be erased from the page of creation?'

The wise monkey's anxieties proved to be correct. One day, the young monkey came up with a new idea; he began to follow the wise farmer, spouting his speech all the while. The wise monkey kept calling after him saying, 'O Young Monkey, why are you bent upon losing your life? Why are you going after a human? Spare a thought for your youth. Save yourself from falling into the endless well of humanity.' But the young monkey did not heed the warning and kept walking on. Out of sheer curiosity, a baby monkey followed him for a long time. The baby monkey returned and told the others how the young monkey had followed the farmer and entered a city of humans and began to walk on two feet and, as he was walking on two feet, his tail got smaller and smaller until it was reduced to a stub.

The wise monkey heard this and, for a long time, sat with his head bent. A fly came and settled on his nose. He sneezed loudly, saw the fly buzzing near his face and opened his mouth wide, then swatted the fly with his paw until finally he grew weary and shut his eyes, and said: 'He went to be with those to whom he belonged.'

The wise monkey opened his eyes after a long time. And when he finally opened his eyes, he saw that the baby monkey had a large piece of paper in his hand and several monkeys were bent over it. Concerned, he asked them: 'O Children of Ill Omen, what is it that you hold?'

The baby monkey answered with a lilt in its voice, 'O Old Monkey, this is a newspaper. I brought this back with me when I went after the young monkey into the city. It carries the testimony of the young monkey.'

The wise monkey heard this and looked in terror at the faces of all the monkeys; he saw that the colour had quite gone from their faces. Then he looked at their tails. He stood up and addressed them thus: 'You ignoramuses, no power on earth can save you from your fate now.'

And with these words, the wise monkey bounded up to the branch of a tree. And leaping from one tree to the next, he went very far away to some other forest. When he disappeared from sight, the monkeys of the Big Forest saw that their tails were becoming smaller and they could no longer walk on all four legs. And then they all climbed down from the trees.

The Last Man[1]

Eleasuf was the last man in the village. He had taken a vow and sworn upon God's name that he had been born in human form and would die in human form. And he tried to remain in human form till the very end.

The monkeys had disappeared from the village three days ago. At first the people were surprised; then they were happy because the monkeys that had destroyed crops and

---

[1] Published as 'Akhri Admi' in the collection of the same name, Lahore, 1967. The names mentioned in this story appear in the Bible. For instance, Eleasuf is a common Hebrew name. Eliazar, another common Hebrew name, was a priest who succeeded his father Aaron and was a nephew of Moses. Zebulun was, according to the Books of Genesis and Numbers, the sixth son of Jacob and Leah, and the founder of the Israelite Tribe of Zebulun. There are at least three individuals with the name Eliab: the son of Helon and a prince of the house of Zebulun according to Numbers 1:9; the son of Pallu and the father of Nemuel, Dathan and Abiram; and the eldest son of Jesse, and thus the older brother of King David. Intizar Husain has used the Arabized versions of these names; I have retained those from the original Urdu.

ruined gardens had left. But the man who used to tell them not to go fishing on the day of the Sabbath told them that the monkeys were still there, in their midst; it was just that people could no longer see them. The people heard him and were offended; they said, 'You jest with us.' But he said, 'Surely you have jested with God for He had forbidden you to catch fish on the Sabbath and yet you went fishing on the day of the Sabbath. And know that He is the greatest jester of all.'

On the third day, it so happened that Gajrum, the slave girl of Eliazar, went to Eliazar's bedroom and immediately turned tail and fled to Eliazar's wife. Eliazar's wife went to his bedroom and was stunned by what she saw. Soon, the news spread far and wide and people began to come from far and near to Eliazar's house. They would go to his bedroom and stand stockstill with surprise when they saw a big monkey resting there instead of Eliazar. On the last Sabbath, Eliazar had caught more fish than all the others.

Soon one person gave the news to the other: 'O Friend, Eliazar has turned into a monkey.' The other laughed loudly and said, 'You are jesting with me.' And he went on laughing, so much that his face turned red, his teeth jutted out, the skin on his face pulled and twisted till he himself became a monkey. Upon seeing this, the first friend was surprised. His mouth fell open, his eyes grew round with wonder and he too turned into a monkey.

Eliab was scared at the sight of Ibn-e Zablun. He said, 'O Son of Zablun, what has happened to you? Why has your face become distorted?' These words made Ibn-e Zablun angry; he began to clatter his teeth with fury. This scared Eliab even more; he shouted, 'O Son of Zablun, may your mother sit in mourning for you! Surely something is wrong with you.' This enraged Ibn-e Zablun even more; his face became red with anger. He clenched his teeth and pounced at Eliab. It made Eliab shiver with fright and the faces of both began to change – Eliab's with terror and Ibn-e Zablun's with anger. Ibn-e Zablun's anger began to cross all limits. And Eliab began to shrink in size with sheer fright. And the two of them – one a statue of anger, the other an emblem of fear – began to grapple with each other. Their faces kept getting contorted. First their limbs became grotesque, then their voices became so distorted that the words kept getting slurred into each other till they became non-verbal sounds. Then the non-verbal sounds became beastly shrieks. And then both became monkeys.

Eliasuf, who was the most intelligent among them and also the one who remained a man till the end, expressed his anxiety thus: 'O People, surely something has happened to us. Let us go and meet the man who used to tell us not to catch fish on the Sabbath.'

Eliasuf went with the people to the home of the man and, standing in a circle before his house, kept calling out to him for a long time. But, when the man did not come out, he was disappointed. He addressed the people in a loud voice: 'O People, the man who used to tell us not to catch fish on the day of the Sabbath has left us and gone away. And if you think about it, it does not bode well for us.' The people heard this and were terrified. They were caught in the thrall of a terrible fear. Terror caused their faces to be flattened, and their skin became coarse. Eliasuf turned to look at them and was shocked. The people walking behind him had turned into monkeys. He looked ahead and saw no one except monkeys. Then, he looked to the left and the right and saw only monkeys in all directions. Scared, he tried to skirt around them and walked from one end of the village to the other.

Let it be known that the village was beside a sea; it had grand houses with high domes and tall gateways. Its markets were crowded and bustling at all times. But within a matter of minutes, the markets were desolate and the houses abandoned. And all around, atop the high domes and the majestic rooftops, only monkeys could be seen.

Dejectedly, Eliasuf turned his gaze in all four directions and wondered aloud: 'Am I the last man left?' And the thought terrified him so much that it nearly caused his blood to freeze. But then he was reminded of Eliab and how fear had caused his face to contort till he had turned into a monkey. Then, Eliasuf sought to gain control over his fear. And he took a vow and swore upon God's name that he had been born in human form and would die in human form. And with a feeling of superiority, he looked upon his fellow beings whose faces had been contorted and said, 'In reality, I am not from among them, for they are monkeys and I was born of human form.' And Eliasuf despised his fellow beings. He looked at their flaming-red faces and their hair-covered bodies, and his face began to contort with disgust. But, suddenly, he was reminded of Ibn-e Zablun whose face had been contorted by disgust and he said to himself, 'Eliasuf, do not despise others for hatred causes man to change his form.' And thus Eliasuf shied away from the feeling of hatred.

And so Eliasuf forsook the feeling of hatred and said to himself, 'Surely, I am one of them.' And then he remembered those days when he was one of them and his heart was overwhelmed with a burst of love. He was reminded of the Prophet Khizr's[2] daughter who was as milky-white as the horse that pulled the Pharaoh's chariot and whose large house had doors made of sard[3] and rafters made of pine. And with that memory came the remembrance of those days when he had entered that house from the rear, whose doors were made of sard and whose rafters were made of pine. And he had gone to the four-poster bed in search of the one his heart longed for. And he had seen the long hair that was damp with dew, the breasts that were aquiver like the young ones of a deer and a belly like a mound of golden wheat with a round bowl filled with sandalwood. And Eliasuf remembered the daughter of Prophet Khizr. And while imagining the young breasts of a deer and the mound of wheat and a round bowl of sandalwood, he reached the

---

[2] Khizr is the name of the prophet skilled in divination who is said to have discovered and drank of the fountain of life; hence he is considered the saint of waters. He is referred to variously as Khwaja Khizr or Ala Khizr. In some parts of the Muslim world, believers make offerings of flowers and lamps to him, placed on tiny rafts that are floated on water.

[3] A sard is an ancient elm, oak, or pine tree that has been infused with lightning.

house with the doors made of sard and the rafters of pine. He looked at the empty house and searched for her on the four-poster bed and called out, 'O daughter of Ala Khizr, where are you? You, for whom my heart longs? Look, the harsh months have passed and the flower beds are full of colours. And the birds are chirping on the high branches of the trees. Where are you, O daughter of Khizr? You who sleep on a high four-poster bed in a high-ceilinged room, where are you? By the deer that frolics in the glades and the pigeons that hide in the crevices of mighty rocks, I beseech you to come down and meet me, for my heart longs for you.' Eliasuf called out again and again until his heart swelled over and, thinking of the daughter of Khizr, he began to cry.

Eliasuf cried as he thought of the daughter of Khizr. But, suddenly, he was reminded of Eliazar's wife who, upon seeing her husband turn into a monkey, had cried. Eliasuf worked himself to such a state that he began to wail inconsolably and his facial features began to contort behind the tears streaming down his face. And his wail turned into a beastly shriek. Even his body began to change. Then he realized that the daughter of Khizr had turned into those she belonged to. For, verily he who is of a certain set will be raised from among his own.[4] And Eliasuf said to himself, 'O Eliasuf, do not love them or else you will turn into them.' And with that Eliasuf turned away from love. He became distant from his fellow beings whom he now considered aliens. And he bid

---

[4] Referring to the Day of Reckoning when the dead shall be raised, each from among his own sort.

adieu forever to the young breasts of a deer and the mound of wheat and the round bowl of sandalwood.

And Eliasuf forsook love and laughed at the sight of the flaming red faces and the erect tails of his fellow beings. And he was reminded of Eliazar's wife who used to be one of the most beautiful women in the village. She was tall and willowy as a date palm; her breasts were like bunches of grapes. And Eliazar had said to her to watch out, that he would pluck those bunches of grapes. And she with those bunches of grapes had turned away and flounced off in the direction of the beach. Eliazar had gone after her and plucked the fruit and brought home the woman who was tall and willowy as a date palm. And now, there she sat on the high branch of a tree, picking lice from Eliazar's body and eating them. A shudder ran through Eliazar's body as he got to his feet and mounted her, his tail erect, his front paws resting on her mangy back as she propped herself on her dirty, limp paws. Eliasuf saw this and laughed, and kept on laughing. And the sound of his laughter grew and grew till the entire village seemed to echo with its sound. And he himself was surprised as to why he was laughing so loudly. Suddenly, he was reminded of that man who had laughed and laughed till he had turned into a monkey. And Eliasuf said to himself, 'Do not laugh at others for you might turn into an object of laughter yourself.' And Eliasuf forsook laughter.

Eliasuf forsook laughter. He then experienced a gamut of emotions – love and hatred, anger and sympathy, tears and laughter – and believing his fellow beings to be alien creatures, he distanced himself from them. Their habit of jumping on trees, clattering their teeth and screeching with laughter, fighting over ripe and unripe fruit till they bloodied themselves – all this used to make him cry over his fellow beings or laugh over them; sometimes it would make him cry or get angry; sometimes he would clench his teeth and look at them with derision.

Once, he saw them fighting among themselves and reprimanded them loudly and then was surprised to hear the loudness of his own voice. A few monkeys looked at him disinterestedly and went back to their fighting. Eliasuf's words ceased to matter, for his relationships with his fellow beings were no longer what they had once been, and this saddened him.

Eliasuf was saddened by his fellow beings, by himself and by the word. He was saddened that for no reason at all they were bereft of the word. He was saddened for himself because the word had been reduced to an empty vessel in his hands. And if one were to think about it, surely today was a sad day, for today the word had died. And Eliasuf mourned the death of the word and fell silent.

Eliasuf fell silent and absolved himself of love and hatred, anger and sympathy, laughter and tears. And he forsook his fellow beings, believing them to be no longer his own, and took refuge in his own self. And taking refuge in his own self, he became like an island: cut off from everyone, a lone speck of land in the midst of deep waters. And the island said to himself: I shall keep aloft the sign of land in the midst of deep waters.

Eliasuf, who well knew the island of his humanity deep

within his self, began to protect himself against the deep waters. He built a bulwark around himself so that love and hatred, anger and sympathy, sorrow and happiness could not attack him, and so that no wave of emotion would sweep him away. And Eliasuf began to be fearful of his emotions. And when he had prepared the bulwark, he felt as though a stone had formed inside his heart. Worriedly, he asked, 'O Lord, am I changing from inside?' And he looked outwards at his body, and he began to feel as though the stone was coming out and spreading all over his body, his limbs were becoming dry, his skin colourless and his blood lifeless. Then he looked closely at himself yet again and once again he was consumed by anxiety. He began to feel as though his body was becoming covered with hair and his hair turning colourless and stiff. And he began to feel as though his arms and legs were becoming shorter and his head smaller. He was frightened even more and his limbs grew shorter still. And he grew scared and wondered: 'Will I disappear altogether?'

And Eliasuf remembered Eliab who had so shrunk within himself with terror that he had turned into a monkey. And he resolved that he would conquer the fear inside himself in the same manner as he had conquered the fear outside him.

And Eliasuf conquered the fear inside him and his shrunken limbs began to stretch out and lengthen. His limbs became supple and his fingers became long and his hair long and straight and his soles and palms grew long and agile and his joints became nimble till Eliasuf began to feel as though his limbs might scatter. With a mighty resolve, he gritted his teeth and clenched his fists and began to collect his scattered self.

Eliasuf closed his eyes so that he would not be awed by his deformed limbs. And when he closed his eyes, he began to feel as though his limbs were changing. Terrified, he asked himself if he was still the same 'I'. The thought made his heart sink. Fearfully, he opened one eye and looked at his arms and legs. He was reassured to see his limbs looking like they always had. Now he opened both his eyes fearlessly and turned a leisurely gaze over his entire body and said: 'For certain I am in my own form.' But soon thereafter, for no reason at all, he began to have misgivings as though his limbs were changing and becoming distorted. Once again, he shut his eyes.

Eliasuf shut his eyes. And when he shut his eyes, his thoughts turned inwards and he began to feel as though he was falling into a dark and bottomless well. He cried out in pain and said, 'O my dear Lord, there is hell outside me and there is hell inside me.' And as he fell into the dark and bottomless well, the faces of his fellow beings followed him and the memories of days long past surrounded him. Eliasuf was reminded how his fellow beings had fished on the day of the Sabbath and how they had emptied the sea of its fish and how their greed had increased and how they had continued to fish even on the day of the Sabbath. And how that man who used to tell them not to go fishing on the day of the Sabbath had said, 'By the Lord who has made the seas deep and made the deep waters sanctuary for the fish, the seas seek refuge from your greedy hands! Beware of inflicting torture on the fish on the day of the Sabbath or else you will be known as those who have brought torture on themselves.'

And Eliasuf had said, 'I shall not fish on the day of the Sabbath.' And Eliasuf who was a wise man had dug a pit at some distance from the sea and connected it to the sea by means of a channel and on the day of the Sabbath the fish came to the surface of the waters, swam through the channel and reached the safety of the pit. And on the day after the Sabbath, Eliasuf caught a lot of fish from the pit. And the man who used to stop people from fishing on the day of the Sabbath, saw this and said: 'He who is deceitful with Allah, Allah will be deceitful with him. And without doubt Allah can be the most deceitful.' And Eliasuf remembered this and became remorseful and anxious. Had he fallen prey to deceit? he wondered. At this instance, his entire life, his very existence, seemed to him nothing short of a deceit. And so he pleaded before Allah, 'O You who have given me life, You have granted me the life that only the Giver of Life can. You created me in the finest mould and made me in Your own likeness. O You who have created me, will you play tricks on me and will you debase me to the order of the lowly monkey?' And Eliasuf began to cry at the sad state of affairs. Cracks began to show up in the bulwark he had built for himself and the waters of the sea began to wash over the island.

Eliasuf cried over his lot and, turning his face away from the habitation of the monkeys, began to move in the direction of the forest, for these dwellings seemed more savage and fearful than the forests, and the house with walls and a roof had lost all meaning for him just as words had lost meaning. He spent the night hiding in the branches of a tree.

When he woke up in the morning, his entire body ached and his spine hurt. He looked at his deformed limbs that appeared more deformed than before. Filled with fear, he asked himself, 'Am I still me?' And in that instant the thought came to him: if only there were one living being in the entire habitation who could tell him who or what he was. And on the heels of that thought he asked himself the question: is it necessary to stay with humans if one wishes to remain a human? And he gave the answer himself: for certain, man is incomplete on his own and one man is tied to another and he shall be raised from among his own lot. And with this thought his soul was filled with anxiety. And he called out, 'O Daughter of Khizr, where are you? For, I am incomplete without you.' In that instant, Eliasuf was besieged with thoughts of those tremulous young breasts of the deer, that mound of grain with the round bowl of sandalwood beside it. The waters of the sea were swamping the island. And Eliasuf cried out in pain, 'O Daughter of Khizr, O you for whom my heart longs, I shall search for you in the four-poster bed in the room with the high ceiling, and in the dense branches of tall trees and amid the lofty towers. In the name of the milky-white mares who run swiftly, in the name of the pigeons that fly in the high skies, in the name of the night when it gets drenched, in the name of the darkness of the night as it descends into the body, in the name of darkness and of sleep and in the name of eyelashes that become heavy with sleep, come to me for my heart longs for you.' And when he made his plaintive call, many of his words jostled with each other like chains that get entangled, like words that get erased, as though his voice was changing. And Eliasuf paused to consider his changing voice and he was reminded of Ibn-e Zablun and Eliab whose voices had become distorted. Eliasuf was scared at the prospect of his changing voice and he thought, 'O Lord, have I changed?' And at that moment the novel idea struck him that if only there was something in which he could see his face. But the thought seemed to be an extremely strange one to him. In pain, he cried out: 'O Lord, how shall I know that I have not changed?'

At first, Eliasuf thought of returning to his habitation. But he became instantly fearful. The very thought of those empty and desolate houses filled him with dread. The tall trees of the forest beckoned him. Dreading the thought of going back to his habitation, he walked far into the forest. When he had walked far, he spotted a lake with placid waters. He sat beside the lake and drank its water and felt relieved. And as he gazed at the pearly water, he was startled. 'Is it me?' He could see his face in the water. He screamed. And Eliasuf's scream terrified him and he fled.

Eliasuf's scream had so terrified him that he began running uncontrollably. He ran as though the lake were following him. As he ran and ran, the soles of his feet began to hurt and seemed to become flat. His back too began to ache. But he kept running. The pain in his back kept increasing till it seemed as though his spine would bend double. Suddenly, he bent and almost unconsciously pressed his palms to the ground. He then shot off on all fours, sniffing the ground for the daughter of Ala Khizr.

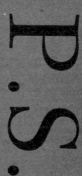 P.S.

The Life and Oeuvre of Intizar Husain

....

Shortlisted for the Man Booker International Prize for 2013, Intizar Husain (b. 1923) has chronicled the changes that unspooled from the Partition of 1947 possibly like no other writer from the Indian subcontinent. Starting his literary career close on the heels of Saadat Hasan Manto (1912–1955), he too has viewed the events of 1947 as an immense human tragedy; however, unlike Manto and the other writers associated with the powerful literary grouping known as the Progressive Writers' Movement, Intizar Husain has shown no predilection for depicting the communal violence that spiralled out of Independence. If Manto probed the horrors of Partition with all the delicacy of a camp surgeon, laying bare a sick, ailing society like 'a patient etherized upon a table', Intizar sahib has chosen to view Partition as hijrat or migration; the greatest cross-border migration in recent history, which he repeatedly likens to a recurrent historical partition, is for him brimful with the possibility of exploring the past while unravelling the present. And so, instead of a compulsive scraping of wounds, a cataloguing of unimaginable horrors and a depiction of a sick, momentarily depraved society that his contemporaries found fit to do as a way of exorcizing the evil within, Intizar sahib has chosen, in story after story, to imaginatively revisit a syncretic, tolerant pluralistic past in a search for meaning, to find out why the tide turned so irreversibly, and why a revisit in real terms often becomes so difficult.

It is only now – close to over thirty years since his first novel *Basti* appeared in 1979 – that the literary world in India is taking stock of his immense contribution not merely to Urdu prose but to a subaltern history. What is more, the Booker shortlist has at long last brought attention to the one overriding concern articulated by Intizar Husain throughout his literary career: namely, the persistent refusal among human beings to learn from past mistakes. For, if there is one overarching theme that strings together Intizar sahib's career as a novelist, short story writer and journalist, it is not merely the haunting sense of loss for a way of life that is irrevocably gone but also a lingering regret. He seems to rue the possibilities that Partition presented but were lost or frittered away. He talks of how, suddenly, almost by accident, Partition allowed writers like him to 'regain' a great experience namely hijrat that has a unique place in the history of Muslims. He even finds a religious sanction for the choice some are forced to make when they leave their homes in search of newer, safer havens. In the story 'Dream and Reality' ('Khwaab aur Haqeeqat'), one of the characters says, 'Friends, remember the hadith of the Prophet: When your city becomes narrow and small for you, you must leave it and go away.' Yet, this unique opportunity too is squandered and the loss makes him sad. As he once said in an interview: 'And the great expectation we had of making something out of it at a creative level and of exploiting it to develop a new consciousness and sensibility – that bright expectation has now faded and gone.'[1]

---

[1] Interview, *Shabkhun*, Vol. 8, No. 96, p. 19.

His epochal novel, *Basti*, is set in 1971 when war clouds are gathering over the subcontinent, the new country of Pakistan is no longer fresh and pure and hopeful but soiled and weary and entirely without hope, and news from distant East Pakistan is ominous. Its protagonist, Zakir, has already faced one tumult, that of 1947, when he left India and migrated to the Land of the Pure. After the first 'luminous' day spent walking the streets of the new city (Lahore) that is to be his home, savouring the delight of walking about freely without the fear that someone will slip a knife into his ribs, soaking in the new sights, sounds and smells, Zakir stays awake all night, weeping and remembering the city, streets, sounds and people he has left behind. 'That day seemed very pure to him, with its night, with the tears of its night.'[2] But those days of innocence and goodness and large-heartedness of the new people in the new land united not so much by one religion but by a common loss and the feeling of homelessness slip away. 'After that, the days gradually grew soiled and dirty. Perhaps it's always like this.' Gradually the goodness and sincerity leach out and in its place there is greed, corruption and intolerance. Looking back, Zakir reflects, 'Those were good days, good and sincere. I ought to remember those days, or in fact I ought to write them down, for fear I should forget them again. And the days afterward? Them too, so I can know how the goodness and sincerity gradually died out from the days, how the days came to be filled with misfortune and nights with ill omen.'

Slowly the vim and vigour of building a new nation begin to sap. Gradually, the cities on both sides of the new border get filled with new people: 'People have come from all kinds of places. Like kites with their strings cut, that go flying and come down on a roof

---

[2] All references to *Basti* are from the translation by Frances Pritchett, Oxford University Press, Delhi, 2007.

somewhere.' So these people, each with their own stories, alight on strange roofs. And speaking through them, in the course of everyday inconsequential conversations, Intizar Husain slips in statements of great import and consequence, and says many things that his own oblique style of storytelling does not allow. For instance, in answer to a question that haunts an entire weary generation of post-1947 Pakistanis: 'Was it good that Pakistan was created?', Intizar Husain makes a wise old Maulvi sahib in *Basti* reply: 'In the hands of the wrong people, even right becomes wrong.' And elsewhere in the novel, there are many seemingly random comments that stay for a long time in the readers' memory: 'When the masters are cruel and the sons rebellious, any disaster at all can befall the Lord's creatures.' Or 'When shoelaces speak, those who can speak stay silent.' Or 'In times such as this, throats become strong and minds weak.' Or, 'Tomorrow might be even worse than today.'

Intizar Husain's stories are cyclical, often stories within stories, replete with anecdotes from the rich oral tradition of storytelling in the Asian subcontinent, scattered with symbols and images that speak more than words. The smell of haarsingaar blossoms, the coming of clouds to a land almost entirely dependent on the monsoon for its yearly supply of water, the strands of flowers covering a groom's face – these are potent images for readers in this part of the world; readily evocative and brimful with meanings, they speak to us across the barriers of language.

'Circle' is, in many ways, typical of his oeuvre. With this story, Intizar Husain has come full circle as a writer too. 'Circle' begins with a reference to a story he wrote fifty years ago, or rather the one he did not quite write the way it ought to have been written: the story that got away! The allusion here is to Intizar Husain's very first story, 'Qayyuma ki Dukan' (Qayyuma's Shop). And now, so many years later, he is compelled to write the story that got away because he has, in his dreams, been scouring his town – the town he left fifty years ago – in search of a person who once used to sit at Qayyuma's shop. Till he has done this, till he has found that person, he is doomed to 'circle round and round forever in a spiral'.

The motif of the circle recurs throughout the story: in a paper kite with its cut string, drifting in a lazy loop of air, in a slowly turning Persian wheel, in a group of children standing in a circle around a snake-charmer and, above all, in a map of Guisetown that begins and ends with Karbala. It is there, also, in the continuing sense of sameness: 'Once again, I have reached there. Once again, I am surprised.'

A dream-like quality pervades much of Intizar Husain's writings. Sometimes it serves not just as a leitmotif, but also as a tool to tell the story in its fullness and rich detail. As he says in 'Circle', 'I do believe that things only reveal their true nature in dreams. Walls and niches, streets and alleys, plants and trees, the earth and the sky – it's only after we stop seeing them with our eyes that we begin to truly see them when they start appearing in our dreams and calling out to us.' Having seen them so often in his dreams, he can now recount every turn in the path that led to the Karbala in his town: the blood-red tamarind tree that grew beside the elephant's grave, the keening of a kite that scratched the air on a hot afternoon more than fifty years ago. The 'scenes' are frozen in time because he sees them so often in his dreams.

Written in a seamlessly flowing narrative style, 'Circle' dips between 'then' and 'now', between 'that' place seen from 'this' distance, between the joys of home and the anguished yearning for home in this transplanted homeland, between sleep and wakefulness. The town of his childhood, which appears in his dreams in myriad guises, is appropriately enough called Guisetown (Roopnagar) in 'Circle'. Occupying a space between the real and the imagined, the town is evoked sometimes with a childlike wonder and sometimes with a near-desperate desire to recount every small detail lest it slip between the crevices of memory and is lost forever. The child of fifty years ago trapped inside him is easily awed: 'What a large, deep pond that was, with steps all around it...'; 'How tall and grand it looks...' and 'Such a crowd of buyers that God save you...' But there is another voice too: '...even though I am one of those who left, all the others have made new homes in new lands. I was the only one who never found peace and tranquillity. Sometimes, I am seized by doubt. Have I left that place or not? ...I am neither here nor there. Like a restless spirit.'

Elsewhere, the dreamlike quality serves to muffle the sense of time and space, making Intizar Husain's stories at once topical and universal – free from their moorings in time, place and circumstance. His characters become Everyman, his context Anywhere where there is strife and turmoil. This is especially true in 'Sleep' and 'Captive'. Sometimes the clue to a story is found in a small, seemingly trivial comment; for example, in 'Captive': 'It's the new definition of captivity', the 'it' referring to friends holding you hostage with their questions, questions which you would rather not answer. To escape that inexorable captivity, Javed, the man who was 'there', who has 'seen it all' asks the most inane and crass questions. For he would rather talk of anything – the newest fashion trends of bellbottoms vs flappers, colourful shalwar suits for men, goggles, lascivious film posters, the delights of Lahore's famed Food Street – anything at all except what he saw 'there'. In the end, there is nothing but confusion confounded. Here – that is, in their own land – there is no sensible answer to be found for the anarchy and bloodshed. 'A man is killed by a bullet, and nothing happens. That's strange, isn't it?' There is no meaning in the loss of innocent lives in a civil society and this indifference to such deaths is what is truly terrifying. That is the difference between 'there' and 'here': 'But at least we knew why it was happening to us … at least we understood what was happening.'

The sense of helplessness, the frustrating inability to find answers to what is happening 'here', as distinct from what happened 'there' recurs in 'Sleep': 'Back and forth, the arguments raged – did people from the other side exploit them or did our own people betray us'. The 'there' in these two instances is Pakistan's deep dark shame: Bangladesh, spawned from the bloodiest internecine war among those who were once brothers. Intizar Husain is among the handful of Pakistani writers who is willing to talk of that national shame, couched in allusions though it is – the 'there' is never mentioned by name. Yet there is no mistaking his deep sense of ownership of that national shame and guilt.

In story after story, there is a deep anguished search for meaning, to hunt for any reason at all to have 'to suffer like this without reason, without cause'. The haunting sense of dislocation, of 'being' yet not 'being' and the unbearable loss of self recurs in most of these stories, most poignantly in 'Those Who Are Lost'. As in *Waiting for Godot,* in this story, too, there is a sense of a search for something indefinable, a lack of something vital that causes the characters to be in a constant state of suspension. As in much of his oeuvre, indeed in his very sense of self, this story is remarkable for the overwhelming sense of loss, of an acute yet indescribable consciousness of the sense of that which has been lost, or left behind.

Another existentialist nightmare is told in 'The Wall'. Interestingly, however, the story – at once timeless and universal – contains a reference to one of the many stories narrated in the Quran, that of Yajoob and Majoob. To my mind, a quintessentially Intizar Husain story, it contains all the concerns that limn his worldview: waiting for something that lies just beyond one's reach, trying to reach the other side knowing full well its futility, the fusing of then and now, here and there.

'Reserved Seat' is a rambling tale about an old woman prone to narrating her dreams in which she sees dead people. It sets itself a slow leisurely pace and catches the reader completely off-guard with its brutal denouement. It carries the vintage Intizar Husain stamp of understatement: a telling comment on the madness that has gripped his homeland, a country where Kalashnikov-wielding Muslims can strike down fellow Muslims praying in a mosque. Through the story of an old woman dreaming strange dreams of long-dead ancestors and living only to see the *sehra* tied on her strapping young grandson's forehead, Intizar Husain makes a powerful comment on the mindless violence of the times he lives in.

'Clouds' and 'Needlessly' stand out from the other tales in this collection for their disarming childlike simplicity. In stories such as these, there is no subtext; they are simple, straightforward and shorn of any literary embellishments whatsoever. Yet they paint charming pictures of wonderment in the simple joys of life.

On the surface, 'Noise' seems to be another simple story like 'Needlessly': two friends set out in search of a quiet spot and walk all across a city that is full of noise; in the end, they return where they started, in a café that is much quieter now and far more conducive to a quiet serious talk about serious matters, but by now the urge to talk has left the two friends. Has the noise in the city numbed their senses, or is it merely a pretext for their unwillingness to talk about dark things? The noise of the city camouflages their dark fears; the city when it falls silent can be a far scarier place than the 'there', the place out there where a war is raging and from where news trickles in only occasionally.

'The Sage and the Butcher' has been chosen for its emblematic quality; it represents the influence of the *Jataka Katha* on Intizar Husain's writings and is one of the vast numbers of stories he has written on incidents and characters from the *Upanishads* and the *Katha Sagar* tradition of storytelling in the Indian subcontinent. I chose to include it here just to give another flavour and to show how Intizar Husain adopts diverse narratorial voices and makes them his own.

'Between Me and the Story' is not quite a story; rather, it is an essay on the acquisition of nuclear arms by the two 'monkeys' in South Asia. A sober reflection on the perils of the atomic bomb in the hands of nations that have not yet grown to full adulthood, it mourns 'life's dark night' that has become 'darker' since the demonstration of nuclear capability. 'The Death of Sheherzad' mourns the fate that befalls all great storytellers when their raison d'etre is taken away from them. The stories dry up on their lips because the wellspring deep within them can no longer sustain creativity.

Then there is the world-weary cynicism of having come full circle to reach one inexorable conclusion: we may have our dreams, but we cannot run away from our destiny. 'Dream and Reality' is a story rooted in the early days of Islam when dreams were pure and untarnished, but despots had already unleashed their reign of terror; the shades of a new homeland for the Land of the Pure talked about in *Basti* are unmistakeable even though the context here is the early years of Islamic history with the mention of real-life characters such as Ibn-e Ziyad. The flight to the safe haven that had been possible in the Prophet's time, now simply brings one back to where one had started. Medina, the City of Light, and Kufa, the City of Darkness, stand out as two poles the human spirit traverses in its search for meaning. Sometimes, when evil has been let loose, this journey becomes not merely hazardous but futile, for as one tries to escape darkness, one simply goes around on a circuitous path from which there is no escape.

Two stories that draw on ancient sources but tell startling modern stories are 'The Story about the Monkeys of the Big Forest' and 'The Last Man'. The former shows a seamless intermingling of snippets from diverse sources that harmoniously come together to tell a cautionary tale: 'This is the tragic tale of the monkeys of the Big Forest, the monkeys that have since disappeared without a trace. The place where the monkeys once lived has turned into a city full of human beings; where there were once tall trees there are now sky-scraping buildings standing in their place. It is said that once upon a time there was a densely forested tract here.' With one story spilling out of the gut of the previous one, quite in the manner of a dastan or qissa, this is as much a story about evolution and change – which can be for good or bad – as it is about the human condition. 'The Last Man' picks up the idea of a man turning into a monkey and brings it to the following, startling conclusion: How does one know that one has changed? What is one's real self? Upon what does one build a sense of being? Does a sense of self derive from the outside world, or does it spring from some unknown well deep inside one?

While the stories included here have been selected not merely for their translatability and innate readability, the fifteen stories have been chosen also to give a glimpse into Intizar Husain's vast and varied oeuvre. That the range of his concerns, not to mention the spatial difference covered in them from the ancient ages through the medieval period to modern times, is eclectic is amply reflected in this selection. Running through all fifteen of them, like the string that keeps the pearls in a necklace together, is Intizar Husain's own voice: measured, mellow and mild, never moralistic or magisterial.

Intizar Husain's writing in Urdu throws up many challenges to the translator. First and foremost, there is the story itself, often not a typical story with a beginning, middle and end, but a rambling monologue peopled by characters from a past that is in many ways more vivid than the present. In other words, not like a story at all but the recounting of a dream, or a story one has heard a long time ago, or maybe in another lifetime. Then there is the simplicity of his Urdu prose, a deceptive simplicity that can trip up the unwary. The cadences that are at once lyrical yet rooted in everyday speech can be amazingly difficult to carry across cultures and languages. Intizar Husain's Urdu is richly textured with both sounds and silences. Often, a great deal is said by what he chooses not to say. Never wasteful with words, he relies on images and motifs that are at once evocative of emotions and feelings: the kite with a cut string drifting past a soot-encrusted crumbling parapet. There is nostalgia, a sense of something irretrievably allowed to slip past and the pain of being severed – all conveyed through a single image. There are short sentences interspersed with long rambling ones with many digressions. There are numerous culture-specific allusions, metaphors and similes drawn from parables, folklore and oral narratives, and images that are immediately and powerfully evocative for a South Asian reader. The rain, for instance, which means totally different things to a child in, say, the UK, and a little boy in the dry dusty plains of north India yearning for the first tumultuous burst of the monsoon clouds. Then there are the bewildering and frequent changes of tense as the stories invariably slip between past and present, between memory and desire. In the best tradition of oral storytelling, craft and technique take a back seat; the spoken word is all.

Then there is his vocabulary. It must be remembered that born as he was in 1923, he spent the first twenty-four years of his life in western United Provinces. The influence of this part of upper India has never quite left him and his writings, even though Lahore has been his home for the better part of his life and career. His writing is replete with references to things that are characteristic to this part of India and to his own Shia Muslim sensibility. The Karbala near his childhood home still exercises a near-magical spell on him.

He can still remember all the lanes and alleys of his neighbourhood just as he can recall the names of the people, not to mention the fruits and vegetables that grew in this part of the world. His language, naturally therefore, has the quaint charm of those long-gone days laced though it is with a simplicity that is the hallmark of the modern and the contemporary.

In translating Intizar Husain, I find it best to stick as close as possible to the 'word' and let the 'spirit' take care of itself. While exact equivalents cannot be found – no two synonyms are quite the same even within the same language – between languages as disparate as English and Urdu, it becomes especially challenging to find resonances that come close to each other. My endeavour in these translations has been to allow the indomitable spirit of Intizar Husain's writing to soar above the translation, intact and unharmed. It is the 'word', the literal text that requires close approximation, and I sincerely hope I have not done an injustice to that.

New Delhi   **Rakhshanda Jalil**
May 2014

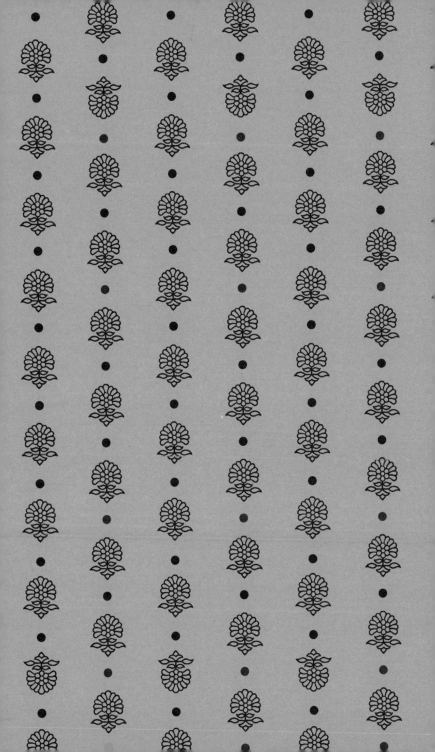